expiration date

expiration date

a novel

SHERRIL JAFFE

THE PERMANENT PRESS
Sag Harbor, NY 11963

For information, address:
The Permanent Press
4170 Noyac Road
Sag Harbor, NY 11963
www.thepermanentpress.com

Library of Congress Cataloging-in-Publication Data

Jaffe, Sherril–
    Expiration date : a novel / Sherril Jaffe.
        p. cm.
    ISBN 978-1-57962-215-2 (alk. paper)
        1. Dreams—Fiction. 2. Death—Fiction.
    3. Fate and fatalism—Fiction. 4. Families—Fiction.
    5. Older couples—Fiction. I. Title.

PS3560.A314E97 2011
813'.54—dc22   2010046218

Printed in the United States of America.

For my mother, Vera Jaffe,
my inspiration and role model,
with love

Chapter One

Flora Margolin Rose, thirty-five years old and almost nine months pregnant, is standing in the prisoner's box. Is that what it's called? "Prisoner's box" is a phrase from a folk song she liked to sing back in the sixties, though she herself was hardly "folk," having been raised in Beverly Hills. The year now on earth is 1980. Flora wonders if this little enclosure which abuts the high bench of the judge might more accurately be described as the "witness stand" or "docket." "Docket" was, after all, the sound of the low wooden gate closing behind her as she entered, though she has no memory of having entered. She only knows she is here, her belly jutting out before her, standing before the cosmic court.

The phrase "prisoner's box" must have entered her mind not because she is a prisoner, but because she is the one standing trial. Flora Rose is on trial for her life. She is not exactly a prisoner. She knows: when this trial is over she will return to earth where things will continue as they were. She will give birth to her baby, and then everything will increase in speed, becoming more and more complex and complicated for the next twenty-five years, and then, finally, her sentence will be executed—she will die.

Flora is aware that she is standing before the heavenly court, though in most respects this chamber resembles a courtroom on earth. The wooden wainscoting gleams. On the wall above it there is a large, round clock, its minute hand racing around its white face, the hour hand jerking forward in pursuit. A calendar hangs nearby, at an angle, as if the wind is moving it up the wall. Its pages lift and flip back, one by one by one by one. On the cream-colored walls above all this hang framed portraits of Washington and Lincoln. Washington looks down upon the proceedings with the rigor of his honesty and his wisdom; Lincoln, with his suffering, bestows compassion and grace. Flora does not

7

question why a courtroom in heaven should have such specifically American icons. Somehow she knows that everything in heaven is absolutely specific to each soul, yet universal all at once. She knows that heaven, the high throne of Truth, has to be entirely paradoxical—paradisical.

The bench of the judge is majestically high. Flora cannot see to the top from whence her sentence is being handed down: this decree that she is to *die*—although not for twenty-five years. Later, after she wakes up and does the math, she will know her death is scheduled to take place some time in her fifty-ninth year, before she turns sixty. She is never to celebrate her sixtieth birthday. But why should the court care about that? Instead, she protests: "I'm about to give birth! I can't die! Who will take care of my daughter?"

Later, of course, she will wonder if this visit to the cosmic courtroom was only a dream, a perfectly understandable nightmare to have when she is pregnant, a time when women often have strange dreams. The pregnancy has, no doubt, imbued her life with a fresh urgency, a new sense of importance. She has a greater reason to live now than she has ever had before—not for herself. She is about to become a mother, a person whose primary function is to nurture, support, and protect her child. She has to stay alive so she can care for her daughter.

Flora knows that the baby growing inside her is a daughter. She had been provided with this information in a dream that was later confirmed by the amniocentesis. In the dream, a dream outside the one she is in now, if this is a dream, a dream which she dreamt on the night of her wedding, the night this baby was conceived, she and Jonah are driving an old pickup truck through the stars. They see a girl hitchhiking and they stop to pick her up. "What's your name?" they ask her. "Lulu," she says, and climbs into the cab. In the morning, the first morning of her life as Mrs. Jonah Rose, Flora awoke with the name "Lulu" on her tongue.

"If we ever have a daughter, what do you think about naming her Lulu?" she asked Jonah. It was almost as if she believed that she would really become pregnant at some point. As it happened,

8

she was pregnant at that very moment, by several hours. They were driving along the Russian River, which, because of the torrential rains the night before, was at its crest.

"Lulu is what they used to call my great-grandmother, Bubbe Ida's mother, Leah," Jonah said. "Shot by the Nazis. They made her dig her own grave."

When Jonah told her this, it became clear to Flora that what she had experienced as a dream had been, in reality, a window into eternity, where Jonah's great-grandmother was passing down her name to them, since it was the Jewish tradition to name children after deceased relatives. The moment of Lulu's conception had provided a portal into a cosmic realm where all of time existed at once, where actions and their consequences were one, where the dead and the not-yet-born reached out to each other.

Sometime during the next week Flora realized there was a strange new taste in her mouth. She went to the doctor, and he confirmed that she was pregnant. This taste was a byproduct of the fact that every system in her body, every fluid and organ, was now dedicated to nurturing Lulu, who was growing inside of her.

It is to her a bizarre and incredible situation—that there could be a person inside of another person. How strange and unfathomable! Lulu is closer to Flora than anyone can ever be, and yet, at the same time, infinitely distant. She is inside of Flora, and yet, they have never met.

Flora can't wait for Lulu to be born so she can look into her eyes and tell her she loves her and that she will be there for her, to take care of her and protect her always and forever. "No, I can't *die*," Flora protests, returning to the Cosmic Courtroom. "My daughter needs me too desperately!"

With infinite patience, the Heavenly Voice replies, "By the time you die, that child will be twenty-five years old, old enough to care for herself."

Flora looks around the courtroom. Will no one come to her defense? There, sitting in a line behind a low wooden balustrade watching the proceedings are her mother, her father, her mother-in-law, her father-in-law, and Jonah's maternal grandmother, Bubbe Ida. Surely they are all on her side; surely they will see the sentence is unfair; surely they will speak up on her behalf!

Flora has only met Bubbe Ida twice—first, shortly after she and Jonah were engaged and he brought her east to meet his family; and then, again, a few months later when Ida came west for their wedding. Yet Flora is certain that Ida really cares for her. When Ida first learned that Jonah and Flora had met and fallen in love, she sent them a generous check to celebrate: she embraced Flora with total acceptance even before laying eyes on her. She just took it on Jonah's say-so that she would love Flora, too.

Flora is glad, because she needs the love of a grandmother. All her own grandparents are dead; indeed, she only knew one of them, Grandma Sadie, her mother's mother, a sad woman who died two years ago. Jonah's grandmother, this frail little woman in her eighties with silver hair braided and pinned around her head, has captured Flora's heart. Bubbe Ida is the perfect grandmother, always knitting. Jonah has two afghans she made for him, and Flora laughingly calls these Jonah's dowry, telling him she would have married him for these alone.

Flora's mother, Muriel, also once knitted an afghan, but only one, when she was pregnant with Flora's older sister, Daphne. Flora loved this blanket when she was little, and she took it with her when she grew up and left home. But along the way a big hole was rent in it by a dog. Flora feels very guilty that she let it be destroyed. It was a treasure from the timeless days of her early childhood when she curled up inside its rosy warmth or crawled inside the floral duvet cover of her parents' satin comforter to watch how the sun shining through the flowers turned the whole world gold.

The last time Flora saw Bubbe Ida was almost nine months ago, after the wedding, when she and Jonah went to say goodbye to his family at the motel where they were staying. It was night, and Ida was already preparing for bed. Her beautiful silver hair was down, and it hung past her waist.

10

As she recalls the scene, tears come to Flora's eyes. Ida is very old, she is clearly living on borrowed time.

Ida glances up from her knitting to meet Flora's gaze. She is sitting behind the low wooden railing, between Beatrice, Jonah's mother, and Jack, Flora's father. Is this the jury box? Is Flora's family here to judge her, or merely to observe, to bear witness? Bubbe Ida sets her knitting down and smiles weakly at Flora, but she does not speak out in Flora's defense.

Nor does Beatrice, Flora's mother-in-law, though Flora is sure Beatrice loves her, too. Beatrice is always offering to do things for her, like help her to set up the baby room. Flora doesn't know anything about baby rooms or baby clothes, or how to put clothes on babies, or how to diaper a baby, but Beatrice is helping her to wash and fold little garments which she has brought for the baby from New York.

Flora does not do much shopping, she never goes to a mall; in fact, she is mildly phobic about malls. She buys all her dresses in vintage clothing stores, but Beatrice is a shopper. Right after they were engaged, when Jonah first brought Flora to Kensico to meet his family, Flora found a large package from a fancy department store tied with a ribbon and laid out for her in the den where they would be sleeping, a welcome-to the-family present from Beatrice. It was then Flora realized how excited Beatrice was that she was coming into the family. In anticipation of her visit, Beatrice had rushed to a department store to get Flora something she thought Flora would really like—a sweater and skirt. She had bought them for Flora sight unseen, and they were a size too small, so Flora had to return them, feeling humiliated. Had Jonah's mother wanted her to be a size smaller than she actually was? The clothes were not to Flora's taste, either; they were much too conventional for her. Did Beatrice want a more conventional daughter-in-law? At that moment she didn't think that she and Beatrice would ever be close.

But then Beatrice had come up to her where she was standing in the living room examining all the art objects displayed on the shelves, and she said, "I'm so happy Jonah found you." She took a small sculpture down from the shelf and cradled it in her hands. It was of a forlorn figure, bent over itself. "This is how Jonah was before he found you," she said, showing it to Flora, implying that Jonah had been lost and hopeless before they met.

But that was not so. Flora would not have fallen in love with Jonah if he had been like this hunched figure. Jonah was great, full, and grand. For a split second Flora felt resentment toward Beatrice for not seeing how powerful and perfect her son actually was.

But that was the last moment of wariness she had with her mother-in-law. Very soon after that Beatrice became to Flora a sort of dream mother, the kind of warm, accepting, uncritical mother she had always wanted to have; the kind of mother who would do anything to protect you, who could summon the strength to lift a Volkswagen off of you if you were pinned under one.

Flora has never really felt this type of approbation from her own mother, Muriel. Indeed, she has often felt like a disappointment to her mother, not entirely worthy of her love. Beatrice and Norman, Jonah's father, drove all the way across country with a car full of baby things in anticipation of Lulu's birth. In so many ways Flora feels championed by Jonah's mother, yet here in the heavenly court Beatrice is not speaking up in Flora's defense, either.

Flora needs someone to come to her defense, because she feels that in twenty-five years she will still be too young to die. She does not need to do the math. "Don't worry about it," Muriel, her mother, pipes up now. "You might not be that old when you die, but you'll *look* old."

That seems to Flora a cruel thing to say, but Muriel often says things that seem cruel to both Flora and her sister, and when they complain about it, she tells them that they are too sensitive—she only wants what is best for them. Still, sometimes Flora wonders if her mother really cares about her welfare at all.

Jack, Flora's father, is in some ways the sweeter parent—or at least, he was. He was the parent who tucked her in at night and told her bedtime stories. He was the one who calmed her when, as a child, she awakened with night terrors. But when she and

12

Daphne were teenagers he showed his rigid, authoritarian side, and then Flora went away to college and never really came back.

Four years later, right after she graduated, when her father was just forty-nine, he had a heart attack on a trip to the Bahamas with her mother. He survived, but he had to stay in the hospital for three weeks to recuperate. Flora flew there to keep her mother company. On the plane, she pretended that her father was already dead to see what that would be like, if it turned out to be the case. But she couldn't feel what it was like to be fatherless beyond this flight—this elevation over the land and then, after changing planes, over the sea.

When she arrived on Grand Bahama Island she found to her relief that her father was going to recover. The trip turned into a kind of vacation. She and her mother soon fell into a routine of visiting her father in the hospital for a few hours of the day, and then going to Happy Hour at one of the hotel bars, eating fried conch and drinking cocktails. In the bars, all of the men flirted with her mother. This surprised Flora. She had not thought of her mother as a woman who was attractive to men before.

That was thirteen years ago. For the past thirteen years everyone in the family has been expecting Jack to die. "Are you alive, Jack?" Muriel is always asking him. It seems to Flora an insulting thing to say to someone, but Jack is impervious to Muriel's insults. In his eyes, Muriel can do no wrong. She is the love of his life, all he has ever really cared about. In some ways, now that his children are grown, he seems to consider himself done with them. So Flora has no expectation at all that *he* is going to speak up in her defense, and he doesn't.

Jonah's father, Norman, also has a Sword of Damocles hanging over his head. He has a chronic stomach condition that was supposed to have killed him years ago. So far, however, he has outlived all of the doctors who gave him his death sentence, but how long can his luck hold? How many more years can her father-in-law live?

Flora knows he will soon be dead, as will Bubbe Ida. Jack and Muriel, her own parents, will also die, without doubt, within the next twenty-five years, before her own expiration date arrives. The little wooden rail all her relatives are sitting behind here in the cosmic courtroom is the demarcation line between *here* and *there*, this world, and the other. In life, none of them has any way of knowing about Flora's expiration date. These things can only be known from beyond the grave, from eternity, where all of time exists in a single moment.

It is of some comfort to Flora to think that her family will be waiting for her when her time comes to cross that line, twenty-five earthly years from now. But it is a common wish, Flora knows, to join with one's dead loved ones in the beyond, so perhaps it is only wishful dreaming to picture all of them waiting for her there. Of course, she also knows that it is just as likely that there is no *beyond,* only dust.

And yet, her family's attendance at the trial where her fate is sealed is in itself proof to her of the reality of the Heavenly Court. It doesn't matter that this courtroom does not seem to have a sapphire floor, the sapphire floor of heaven that Flora has glanced up to see as a ceiling above her all her life.

Or is the floor made out of sapphires? Flora does not know, because she does not look down. She stands in the prisoner's box receiving her sentence, and she wonders if everyone on earth, at some point, is afforded such a glimpse of heaven as she is being granted; if each soul during the course of its life is transported for a brief visit to this courtroom in the supernal realm to stand trial and hear its expiration date proclaimed. And afterwards, when returned to earth—where no time at all had elapsed—if an angel touches each person's eyelids, so that everyone forgets or disbelieves what they have just heard: the proclamation of the day of their death.

Even though not one of them speaks in her defense, Flora cannot fault her dear relations, all sadly fated to precede her in death, for not standing up for her. After all, a heavenly decree is a heavenly decree, and there is nothing one can do in the face of it.

Is there?

Is there *nothing* one can do?

Chapter Two

Muriel Margolin sat at the foot of her husband's hospital bed as he lay dying. Could this actually be happening? She was numb.

At the head of the bed stood Emilio, who had been Jack's live-in nurse ever since the open-heart surgery four years before, in 2000. The operation had repaired Jack's heart, but he awakened from the anesthesia delirious. When the delirium subsided they found he had become incontinent and had lost the use of his legs. Muriel was sure that they didn't give him enough oxygen during the surgery, and that was why this had happened. Jack was old, eighty-five, and because he was old, they probably thought he wasn't worth bothering with.

Muriel had wanted to sue, but she was too overwhelmed with trying to care for her suddenly incapacitated husband to follow through. Luckily, the hospital gave her a list of registered nurses for hire, and that was when she found Emilio. He never left Jack's bedside in the hospital, and he came home with them to Beverly Hills when Jack was released.

When it became clear that Jack would never walk again, Muriel decided to move to the Bay Area to be closer to her younger daughter, Flora, who lived with her family in San Francisco. Muriel's older daughter, Daphne, with whom she was actually closer, lived in Portland, but it was too cold and rainy for Muriel to consider moving there. Both she and Jack had been born in Los Angeles and they had lived there their entire lives. They weren't used to cold weather.

Although Muriel wasn't particularly close with her younger daughter, Flora was the sensible one, and besides, she had a responsible husband, a rabbi, who could be counted on in an emergency—and Muriel knew more emergencies were coming.

She had already survived a bout of breast cancer, and although she was in good health now, it couldn't be much longer before she would need to be taken care of herself.

Actually, she had wanted to move for some time, but Jack would never agree to it because he didn't want to leave the house they had built when their family was young. But now that he was confined to a wheelchair and had retreated into himself, hardly speaking at all, he couldn't protest when she put the house up for sale and bought a brand new three-bedroom condominium in Laurel Dell, a retirement community in Walnut Creek. She wasn't really sure that he understood what was happening.

Luckily, Emilio agreed to move with them. The man was a saint. Muriel didn't know what she would have done without him. He was fifty years old and didn't mind leaving his wife behind in Los Angeles. He was taking all his pay and putting it into a house he was building in the Philippines, where he was planning to retire. It seemed to Muriel that all Filipino people had exceptional characters. They honored and respected their elders; they didn't just assume that people were worthless, ready to be thrown on the junk heap once they reached a certain age. He took excellent care of Jack, and Jack was extremely attached to him.

Without Emilio, Muriel would have had to put Jack in a nursing home. She couldn't have handled him on her own. Jack was a big man, a tall man, and Muriel at five-foot-two and 112 pounds wasn't strong enough to lift him from his wheelchair to the hospital bed they had brought home with them. The bed was outfitted with a constantly inflating and deflating mattress, and Jack lay on it contracted, unable to straighten his legs, listening to the books on tape Muriel rented for him from the Society for the Blind.

Once they were settled in Walnut Creek, Muriel bought a wheelchair-accessible van, and the three of them went out to dinner, and to Macy's, and to the movies, and to San Francisco on Sunday mornings to have brunch with Flora and her family at their favorite restaurant, Greens. The condominium was new and

16

fresh, with a view of Mt. Diablo. Emilio slept in one bedroom, Jack's hospital bed was set up in another, and Muriel had the master suite to herself.

Emilio would put Jack into bed fairly early, and then Muriel would come in and kiss him goodnight. He was so sweet, it almost broke her heart. But then, as soon as Jack was asleep, Muriel would go out to play bridge. Bridge was her passion, and had been for the past thirty years. She was a Life Master many times over and loved to play in tournaments. With Emilio living with them, she was able to go out at night, and she could also take short trips to tournaments in different cities around the country, and life wasn't so bad.

But now all this was ending. Jack was dying. He had aspirated his food and now he had pneumonia. His body had lost its ability to distinguish which pipe was for food and which for air, and there was no way to repair this. They had put him on a morphine drip: it was just a matter of time.

Muriel sat and watched the morphine dripping into him through the tube. She looked at all the machines behind his bed with their lights and screens. She hated this hospital. Bile rose in her throat.

People who went into this hospital never came out. During the four years they had been in Walnut Creek, Muriel had lost several dear friends to this hospital. The first was Trude, a lovely woman, the first new friend Muriel had made in Laurel Dell. They had been bridge partners, and then they started taking BART together to go to the symphony in San Francisco. Being with Trude had helped Muriel get used to this strange new place, and then one day Trude went into this hospital and she never came out.

Another friend lost to this hospital was Dick, whom Muriel had met in her morning exercise class, where he always stood behind her. Muriel was proud of her trim figure, and she knew Dick found her attractive; and sometimes, after Jack was asleep at night, they went out to dinner together. She was married, of course—they were just friends. But he was a tall, attractive man, and she thought that when Jack died—and how long could he go

17

on in his condition?—that she would have Dick as a companion. Then one day Dick went into this hospital and that was the end of him. This hospital killed everyone who came near it! After today, Muriel vowed, she would never come near this place again.

Yet, what was to become of her? She had married Jack when she was only twenty. How could she begin a new life now at age eighty-five?

She hadn't wanted to marry Jack. In fact, she had returned his ring to him twice, but her father had forced her to take it back again. Her father didn't want to support her anymore. Muriel had a boyfriend with a sailboat, and she loved sailing with him and going to dances. Then he went away to medical school. There was the Depression on, and Jack would be a good provider, Muriel's father told her. He wasn't what she wanted in a man: he didn't sail and he didn't dance. But Jack was a good man, an honorable man, and he did provide for her, and he loved her. He adored her, he worshipped the ground she walked on, and she came to care for him, too. How could he desert her, now? What was she going to do?

Their daughters stood, one on either side of Jack's bed, holding his hands. When they learned the end was near, Muriel had Flora call Daphne and tell her to come down. There had been a slight argument. Daphne had said, "Why don't I just come down for the funeral? Why make two trips?" and Flora had been rather sharp with her. "Come down, now!" she said. "You'll want to be here!" So Daphne came, and she apologized to Flora, telling her she was right. She wasn't thinking. She didn't think straight in emergencies.

Her daughters didn't listen to her. Muriel had given up trying to give them advice. They always thought she was criticizing them. She looked at them, both huddled over their father. She wished they would stand up straight. There were so many old people in Laurel Dell, this strange community she had moved to, people who walked with a stoop or had humpbacks. If they had only practiced standing up straight before it was too late, they would be a lot better off. Muriel was always reminding herself to stand up straight, and so far she had no sign of a hump, even though she was eighty-five. But what would happen to her daughters? Daphne was already in her sixties and Flora was in her fifty-ninth year. What was going to become of them?

"I love you, Dad!" Flora said. "I love you, Dad!" Daphne said, but Muriel couldn't speak. She was paralyzed and numb.

Jack's eyes were open. There was an expression of wonder—or was it terror?—on his face. He looked like he was peering out into the beyond. Was there a beyond? Jack was not religious—he had no belief in any sort of afterlife, but he always liked to ask questions like, "What is beyond the furthest reaches of the universe? What is at the end of time?" Muriel was not religious, either, but she was glad Flora's husband, Jonah, was there. They wouldn't have to worry about finding a rabbi to do the funeral.

Her own mother had died before Jonah was in the family, and they'd had to look up a rabbi in the phone book. He turned out to be a short, unpleasant man, and since he had never met Sadie, her mother, the service he performed was totally generic. All that he said of a personal nature was that Sadie was a good housekeeper.

Muriel must have told him that herself, of course. But did she tell him that her mother scrubbed the kitchen floor so vigorously that the pattern was rubbed away? Did she tell him that the four of them all used the same bathroom because her mother didn't want to have to clean two bathrooms? At the funeral the rabbi read something about a woman of valor, also. It was all so sanctimonious. Muriel's mother had been an obsessive housekeeper, that was true, but she certainly wasn't a woman of valor.

She had almost no valor at all, as far as Muriel could tell. Muriel's father had died of a heart attack when he was forty-eight, so her mother was widowed when she was only forty-nine, and then she simply gave up on life. She lived on her husband's life insurance payout for the next thirty-five years, doing nothing, first in a studio apartment, and then, after her suicide attempt, in a series of retirement and nursing homes. Muriel went to see her every week, bought her underwear and took her out to lunch, but nothing made her happy. Sadie had a series of suitors, who gave her bottles of perfume, and these bottles were lined up on her dresser, but they were never opened. Muriel watched her mother reject each suitor. Sadie was afraid they were after her money.

Jack was now taking long drawn-out breaths. He was leaning forward in the bed, his eyes fixed on something Muriel couldn't see.

Just then the door to the room opened and Flora's daughters, Lulu and Posey, burst in. "Sorry we're late," Posey said. "They wouldn't let us into the parking lot. A helicopter was landing." The girls went to either side of Jack's bed, and Daphne and Flora stepped back. "I love you, Grandpa," they kept saying. Daphne had two daughters, too, but they lived too far away to get here on time.

Jack had always enjoyed being surrounded by females. One of the reasons Muriel wanted to move here was so she could get closer to her granddaughters. It was hard to believe that Lulu was already twenty-four. When Muriel was twenty-four she had already been married four years. But girls didn't have to get married right away anymore. They could have a life.

But what would happen to Muriel? She had never lived alone. She had gone from her father's house to her husband's, and now what was she going to do? She and Jack had lived most of their lives together. When he was gone, she would be the sole repository of the memory of everything they had experienced over all these years. He was the youngest of seven siblings, and they were all dead now, too. And Muriel's only brother was dead. Dead, dead!

Who would be there to kiss goodnight and say "I love you" to? What would become of all their private jokes, their special language? How could she continue to live without this one person who treasured her above all others?

What was going to happen to her? Even Emilio would leave her. Then she would be alone in this strange place, Walnut Creek. It was so different here, so unlike anything else she had ever known. Her father had been right about one thing. Jack had been a good provider. If she was careful, her money could last her quite a long time.

Jack's breaths became more labored. "I love you, Grandpa," Lulu was saying. Jack expelled one last long breath. It seemed to go on forever.

But then he was still, his eyes fixed.

His color went from pink to white and then to yellow.

Emilio bent over him and closed his eyes.

EVERYONE IN the room, except for Muriel, was gathered around Jack. Muriel still sat in her chair, at the foot of his bed. She was now a widow, like her mother before her.

She had been expecting to become a widow ever since Jack's heart attack in the Bahamas, thirty-eight years ago. She had been expecting it, but at the same time, when it didn't happen, she had also started to believe that it would never happen. When Jack had his open heart surgery she thought again it was going to happen then. But he had lived on, and Emilio had taken such good care of him; and after they moved to Walnut Creek they got into a routine—going to the movies, to Macy's, to Greens on Sunday mornings—it seemed like it could go on forever, though at the same time Jack was withdrawing from her little by little, contracting. He sat with his head down in his wheelchair pushed up to the kitchen table, and Emilio placed a rubber ball in his contracted hand and said, "Squeeze it, Jack," tying a bib under his chin so that he could be spoon-fed while doing his exercises. Jack gave the ball a little squeeze. "Put your head up, Jack," Muriel said, "Look at me," and he raised his head a little bit, and his eyes twinkled at her, and then he let his head fall again, and she knew she was saying goodbye to him every night, kissing him goodnight and telling him she loved him.

Had it really happened?

Was it real?

Muriel's mother had lived on her husband's life insurance policy for thirty-five years after he died, and, oddly enough, Sadie herself had died on the very day that the money was finally all used up. Time was money, apparently, and Muriel had plenty of money; therefore, she had plenty of time.

But what was she going to do with it? She knew she was an old woman, but she didn't feel like an old woman. She just felt like herself, the same person she had been since she was a child, since the day her bulldog followed her to school and the teacher made her bring him home, where she found both her mother and the maid on the floor, scrubbing the linoleum, and her little brother running in circles, holding his model airplane aloft. But now she had no mother, no brother, no children to raise, no husband to care for.

She looked at her daughters hovering in grief above their father's yellow corpse.

No one even seemed to notice she was there, at the foot of the bed.

Jack was dead at last, but she was still alive!

Chapter Three

The phone was ringing, and when the phone rang Flora always felt a *frisson* of fear. It had been that way for her entire life. She remembered being very small and her mother giving her instructions in how to answer the phone, and how terrified she was that she would have to actually do it.

Flora had been peeing when the phone started ringing. After she pulled up her pants and washed her hands, she stood looking down at the machine. The caller ID said "Out of the area," so she surmised it was a telemarketer calling to sell her something and she decided not to answer. But what if it wasn't a telemarketer? What if it was Jonah? He was out of the area, in New Jersey visiting his sister. She picked up the receiver on the fourth ring. "Hello?" she said.

"Good morning! Is Mrs. Flora Rose there?" an unfamiliar male voice asked.

"I'm sorry, she's not," Flora lied. "Would you like me to give her a message?"

"Yes, tell her John Lancaster called from the Alameda County Sheriff's Office."

"I'll tell her," Flora said.

Her first assumption upon hearing the word "sheriff" was that one of them—she or Jonah or one of the kids—was in trouble with the law, and this thought made her heart leap temporarily into her throat. But then reason took over and she realized that the sheriff was only trying to sell her raffle tickets.

The sheriffs intimidated her into buying raffle tickets every year. She bought them out of fear, thinking the law would find a way to get back at her if she didn't. She resented being manipulated in this way, and a few years ago she started making Jonah take these calls. Talking to the sheriffs didn't bother him. He was always polite in his dealings with them. Every time they called he would cheerfully agree to buy several of their raffle tickets. "Just send me the bill," he would tell them.

After a while, the bills would arrive, but he would never open them. He never gave them a penny for their raffle tickets. Flora was afraid that the sheriffs and the firemen—who also solicited money from them in this way—would get really mad and take revenge upon them once they realized that Jonah wasn't sending them the money he promised. But strangely enough, they didn't seem to notice that he never sent them anything. They just kept calling, they kept asking for donations, and they never once mentioned the outstanding bills. "Would you like to pledge the same amount, send the same number of orphans to the circus?" a deep male voice would ask, and Jonah would say he would do the same thing he did last year, and he did.

"I'll tell her you called," Flora said now, lying bravely to the sheriff. But, after all, what could he say? You're lying? I know *you're* Mrs. Rose? She might go to jail for lying to a sheriff, but she was willing to risk it. It was now September, one month into her fifty-ninth year, her last year on earth—at least that was what, on some level, she continued to think—and since she might have very little time left, she didn't want to squander it by acting out of fear.

Jonah continued to pooh-pooh the idea that she knew her expiration date, even though he thought he knew *his*. He was convinced he would die when he turned sixty-seven, at the exact age his father and both his grandfathers had died. Never mind the recent studies which showed the age one's parents died in no way predicted when one would go; never mind the fact that his father had had a chronic stomach ailment which Jonah didn't have; never mind the fact that his maternal grandfather died of leukemia brought on by exposure to benzene which Jonah was never exposed to; and never mind the fact that in talking with a cousin recently he learned that his paternal grandfather had actually died shortly after his *seventieth* birthday, Flora knew Jonah would never breathe freely until he woke up alive on his sixty-eighth birthday, in seven years, as she would not let out her breath until she woke up alive on the morning of her sixtieth birthday, in eleven months.

While she was still standing by the phone it rang again. This time it was Jonah, Flora saw, reading his cell phone number on the caller ID, and she answered. He was calling from his sister's house. They had just gone together to visit their parents' graves. The cemetery was located close to Paramus, where people from all over went to shop in the big malls to avoid paying tax. If it was true that the only things that could really be counted upon were death and taxes, and if the shopping center in Paramus disproved half this adage by having no tax, did the cemetery nearby disprove the other half of the adage, the part about death? It must have seemed that way before Jonah's grandfather, Joe, was planted into its soil. The cemetery was brand new then and practically empty. Now it was a veritable necropolis. Jonah's grandmother and both his parents were here now, too, and the whole cemetery had filled up with headstones surrounding theirs.

"We visited Beatrice and Norman first," Jonah told Flora. "I can't believe that my father's been dead more than twenty years already!"

Flora thought back to that time of their family's life, and she remembered how Norman had hung around doing mischief for a year after he died. Lulu was three, then, and she talked about her *zayde* every day of that year of mourning, and Flora had been sure that it was because Norman was prodding her to remember him from the grave. This made Flora very angry at him. Lulu was having nightmares every night because of him. He was being selfish in the extreme. It might be terrible to die and have all memory of your existence fade from the earth, but to indulge your ego at the expense of the peace of mind of an innocent child was simply unconscionable. Lulu was shaken for that entire year; and though they took her to a counselor and read her books which were supposed to help her adjust to the idea of death—books about leaves falling from trees, showing how beautiful and natural and not scary death was—nothing helped. Lulu continued to have night terrors and to talk about her grandfather. He wouldn't leave her alone. Flora imagined herself in a cosmic battle with Norman as she tried to protect her daughter. Then, at the end of the year, for no apparent reason, he finally went away.

Jonah's mother, Beatrice, died twenty years later, after a long siege with Alzheimer's, but she didn't cause any trouble after she died. Perhaps it was not in her nature to do so, or maybe the Alzheimer's, which had been a sort of death-in-life, had made her less restless when she was finally in her grave.

"Did you have a nice chat with your parents?" Flora asked. She knew Jonah would try to commune with them. According to Jewish lore, the soul had many levels, and one level, the lowest and most primitive, always stayed with the body. She knew Jonah believed this.

"They weren't too communicative today," Jonah said. "So we just put rocks on their headstones and went to pay Ida and Joe a visit."

Jonah's Bubbe Ida had died only a few months before his father. Beatrice had lost both her mother and her husband within a space of months. Flora shuddered to think how terrible that must have been for her. After Bubbe Ida died, Flora remembered, the whole family convened in her apartment in Manhattan Beach every evening for a week, for a *shiva minyan* to say the afternoon service together so the mourners could say *kaddish*, the prayer for the dead. On the first night, Flora went into Ida's bedroom to nurse baby Posey so they wouldn't disturb the service going on in the living room. She found two of Jonah's second cousins, middle-school girls, already taking refuge in there. They were sitting on one of the twin beds, whispering. Flora sat down on the other. Both beds were made with matching bright orange bedspreads. Between the beds was a table upon which stood a large lamp radiating a pleasant glow. Flora put the baby to her breast.

As Posey suckled and stared into Flora's eyes, Flora listened through the wall to the drone of the service in progress in the living room, and soon she heard the familiar insistent rhythm of the *kaddish* being intoned by the mourners. It was then, during the recitation of this ancient Aramaic tongue twister, that the lamp on the table between Ida's beds started to flash on and off. Jonah's cousins looked at each other with wide eyes and then at Flora to see if she had noticed, to see if she, too, thought Ida was communicating with them through the lamp.

Years later, when the cousins had grown into young women, Flora would ask them if they remembered when this happened. They didn't, they would say, and Flora would wonder if an angel had come and touched each of them lightly on the eyes, causing them to forget.

Later that same week, the week of Ida's *shiva*, Jonah and Flora were sitting on the blue couch in their apartment on the Upper West Side near the seminary where Jonah was going to school, when a book fell out of the bookcase on the opposite wall. Flora got up to put it back. It was *Ida*, by Gertrude Stein. Bubbe Ida was saying hello to them! After that, she disappeared. But where did she go? Was she still herself, wherever she was? What lay ahead, through that door, over the horizon?

I'll soon know, Flora thought, as she said goodbye to Jonah and hung up the phone. There were only eleven months to go before her expiration date when this mystery would be solved for her. Of course, if when she died it turned out that she became nothing, nothing would be revealed. It was fruitless to try to guess at what lay ahead. What will be revealed after we die will be nothing like what we have imagined, Heraclites had said.

She thought about how when her own father had died, he also had hung around for a little while, doing mischief—to chastise her for her failures as a daughter, perhaps, or maybe just to get a final bit of attention. On the way back from his funeral in Los Angeles she had noticed that her wallet was missing. She was always careful of her wallet, it was not like her to lose it. She blamed her father as she went through the hassle of getting a new ID. Her father's death had changed her identity, and he clearly wanted her to be aware of it. In addition, when they arrived home, they found the large dish that hung over the mantle in the dining room had fallen off the wall and shattered into a thousand pieces. Flora had loved that plate, and she was sure her dead father had smashed it to let her know how death was real, that eventually everything fell, smashed, and broke. Or maybe he had done it simply out of anger over being dead. She didn't know.

Flora thought how the only parent she and Jonah had left now was Muriel, but Muriel seemed like she was going to be around for a long time. She was in incredible shape. People were always saying to Flora, "This is your mother? I thought she was your sister!" and Flora would answer, "Thanks! Do I look like I'm in my eighties?" And then she would remember what Muriel had said to her in the Cosmic Courtroom: "Don't worry about being too young to die—you'll *look* old!" And then people would say, "Oh, no, you don't look like you're in your eighties, it's just that your mother looks so young!" Later when she told him about it, Jonah would reassure her that she did look young, and he would tell her that she was beautiful, too. But she knew age was starting to take its toll on her—and on Jonah, too. His hair was almost all gray now; and sometimes, in a certain light, when she looked at the skin on her inner arm it looked like crepe.

Crepe is what one wore for mourning.

Flora remembered the first time she realized that her parents were aging. She must have been about twelve and her mother only thirty-nine then, her father forty-three. Flora had walked into their bedroom for some reason and found them sitting in the half-light of the TV, and she suddenly saw their chins were sagging and their stomachs were protruding. Their aging was horrific to Flora, and not a little repulsive. She remembered thinking then that her parents would soon be dead and she recalled how frightening that thought was.

For most of her life she had been terrified of her parents dying, even when she felt most disregarded by them and thought that she was wishing for it.

She remembered that once, when she was about the same age, her parents went out for the evening, telling Flora when they'd be home. Her sister was at a friend's house, and Flora waited up for her parents, but they didn't come home when they said they were going to. As the clock ticked on she became more and more convinced they had been killed in a car accident. She sat paralyzed with fear. But when they finally walked in the door she wasn't glad to see them, she was furious at them for making her worry.

As Flora laced up her sneakers in preparation for her morning walk, a walk she took every day in spite of the fact that on some level she didn't think it would extend her life, she thought about how she had just lied about her name to the sheriff, and she remembered what Jonah had told her about the old Jewish trick of avoiding the Angel of Death by changing your name. When the Angel came knocking on your door asking if Mrs. Flora Rose was home, for example, you could make him go away by saying, "I'm sorry, there's no one by that name here, only a woman named Alter-Flora Rose."

When Flora arrived at the polo field, she started to circle it, as she did every morning. In the center of the field was a man she had seen many times before, a professional dog walker, she assumed, because he always had about ten or fifteen dogs of every sort, shape, and size with him. Today he had a golden retriever, two corgis, a beagle, a basset hound, a black Lab, an Australian shepherd, a Jack Russell terrier, a bulldog, and several other dogs, both large and small. Some were chasing balls he lobbed for them, some were retrieving Frisbees, and some were running toward him with sticks in their mouths. One was running madly in circles, two were tussling with each other, and several others were sitting facing the man with rapt attention. All were clearly hyper-aware of this man, who continuously called to each of them: "Tyler! Tyler! Heidi! Rollo! Barkley!" It made Flora smile to see them, the dogs all so obviously glad to be under the man's beneficent control. It was so wonderful how he could look after them all at once, giving each such loving attention, giving each dog what each dog needed, like a good father. Tears began to well behind her eyes. She had no father anymore.

Flora always took the same route on her walk through Golden Gate Park. On weekdays, in the mornings, she was almost the only one on the path. But on Sundays, and today was a Sunday, there were often events set up along her route past Speedway Meadow. Today she saw a horde of people in pink tee-shirts with pink ribbons pinned to them walking toward her as she headed down the hill, so she knew it was a breast cancer event, perhaps a marathon, though no one seemed to be running. A stream of pink-clad people were coming up through an archway made out of pink balloons. These were all people who had breast cancer, or who had someone in their family or a friend with breast cancer. Flora knew quite a number of people who had it. Her own mother had had breast cancer. Muriel had had a mastectomy and then reconstruction and seemed to be fine, now. The reconstruction had been so successful, in fact, that at her last mammogram the technician had mistaken it for a real breast.

Flora, as it happened, didn't have breast cancer. Not yet, as far as she knew, though something was going to be the cause of her death sooner or later; and she, of course, was convinced it would be sooner, and now she was walking amongst the pink-shirted people as if she were already one of them.

Portable toilets lined the path. A stage had been erected in the meadow. Arabic music poured from the sound system, and now Flora saw there were belly dancers on a stage. Women in pink tee-shirts with pink ribbons were standing in the field between the pavilions, moving their hips from side to side to the music: being alive, being supportive of each other. Flora passed a group of people—many of them men—all wearing the same black tee-shirt with a photo of the same woman silk-screened on the back. Flora wondered if they were all friends of a certain woman who had breast cancer, and to show their support for her they all had her picture silk-screened to their shirts; and Flora wondered if this was a picture taken of her before or after chemotherapy, and if she was dead.

She passed into an avenue of trees, and suddenly there were no other people on the path. She could still hear the belly-dancing music—faintly—and then, out of the bank of trees where she often saw dishes left out for feral cats and had once glimpsed a rat disappearing, she heard music emanating from what must have been a boom box someone was playing up in the brush: an excited woman's voice was singing, "I will survive! I will survive!"

But the voice was disembodied, and there was no one there.

Chapter Four

Muriel sat in the waiting room of the clinic attached to Laurel Dell. Her appointment was for 9, and it was already 9:15, but they didn't mind keeping old people waiting. They assumed old people had nothing better to do than to sit in waiting rooms at doctors' offices. When her mother was old—or when Muriel had thought she was old—Sadie had endless doctors' appointments. Sadie was always running to doctors, and Muriel was always busy driving her to these appointments. Sadie complained constantly that her nerves were bothering her, but everyone knew she was a hypochondriac. The doctors never found anything wrong with her, but they gave her endless prescriptions for pain medicines, nonetheless. She became addicted to the pills, and one day she took a whole bottle.

Muriel and Flora were the ones who discovered her in the midst of her suicide attempt. They had come to pick her up for Flora's sweet sixteen party, and when she didn't answer the door, they called the fire department. They found her in her bed with her hands clutching the iron bedstead. She was breathing erratically, and she wouldn't wake up. The firemen came and carried her out, knocking her knees together, and she had deep purple bruises on the inside of her knees for a long time afterwards. The firemen took her to the hospital where they pumped her stomach, and saved her life. Afterwards, Muriel and Flora went to the party at the restaurant, Scandia on the Sunset Strip, where everyone was waiting. They had to, really.

It was because of her mother's example that Muriel hardly ever took pills herself. They wanted Muriel to take Tamoxifen after her breast cancer was treated, and she pretended that she would. But she read the insert that came with the medicine, and

32

there were too many side effects. And they wanted her to take Lipitor for her cholesterol, which was a bit too high, but that also had terrible possible side effects, so she never refilled that prescription, either—though she pretended to her doctor that she was taking that, too. "Mrs. Margolin, you could live to 110," her doctor always said to her. "And just why would I want to?" she always replied.

Lately they had started insisting she take Fosamax for her bones, so she agreed, and pretended to take that, too. She would take a daily walk for her bones. The purpose of getting everyone to take all these medicines, she was sure, was to make the drug companies rich. It made her angry even to think about it. The only pill she took was a little one, for her blood pressure. She was getting angrier and angrier sitting here waiting for the nurse to decide to allow her to see a doctor who probably was quite mediocre. If he were any good, why would he waste his time with a bunch of old people?

There was another woman in the waiting room with her, a white-haired woman with a walker who seemed to be wearing a bathrobe. She was screaming "Nurse! Nurse!"

"I know you're here, Mrs. Gevurtz," the nurse said in an overly loud, fake-pleasant voice. "But your appointment's not until ten. Your driver brought you too early! You'll just have to be patient."

Muriel wondered how old Mrs. Gevurtz was. She hoped *she* never got that old. If she did, she hoped Flora would have the good sense to shoot her. No, it couldn't be Flora. Flora was a pacifist. Flora hated guns. It would have to be the other daughter. She was more malleable.

"Nurse! Nurse!" Mrs. Gevurtz called again, in a booming voice.

"We know you're here, Mrs. Gevurtz," the nurse said loudly, once more, though this time not so pleasantly.

The reason Muriel was here was simply for a checkup. She would need one if she applied to live at the Bradshaw, the senior residence in San Francisco Flora was going to take her to see. She had to get out of Laurel Dell. She felt dead there.

When she had walked into the doctor's office, the nurse had given her a questionnaire on a clipboard to fill out. She was half finished with it. One of the questions was if she had had any surgeries. She'd had only two, her mastectomy and—she glanced down at the scar on her right arm—a lipoma, a fatty tumor, which had been removed by an orthopedic surgeon. It was perfectly harmless, benign.

The form asked for the date of the surgery. It was years ago—in fact it had to have been 1980, twenty-four years ago now, because she remembered the day she noticed it in her arm. She and Jack had driven up to San Francisco where she went to a bridge tournament they had at the Palace Hotel every year. Jack had some business to do in the city. One day they picked up Aunt Libby, who lived in Oakland then, and they went to visit Flora and Jonah. The kids packed a lunch, and they all drove to a redwood forest to have a picnic. Flora was very pregnant with Lulu then—that's how she could place the date: Lulu was now twenty-four. She remembered carrying part of the picnic so her pregnant daughter wouldn't have to, when she noticed her wrist was aching. She looked down and saw there was an enormous lump in her forearm.

When she got home, she went right to the doctor, and he sent her to the orthopedic surgeon to have it removed. It was only a fatty tumor, nothing to worry about.

After that, Aunt Libby moved to Connecticut. That was where her only son, Muriel's cousin Jimmy, lived with his second wife. Libby moved at Jimmy's urging. He found her an apartment in an old age home where she got all her meals. She was eighty-four, younger than Muriel was now, but Muriel had thought her so old!

She and Jack visited her in Connecticut the following year. The place was strange, so stark, in the middle of nowhere, and Libby said she couldn't get used to it after living in California all her life. "How is the food?" Muriel asked, and Libby said "I don't know." Her taste buds had stopped working, she had lost her ability to taste.

34

"She's lost her taste for life," Flora said, when Muriel told her about it. Flora was always interpreting everything, reading into things. But it was soon clear that it was a mistake for Libby to have moved to Connecticut. Shortly after she got there, her daughter-in-law had a dinner party and didn't invite Libby. When Libby asked her son why, he explained to her that his wife had forbidden Libby to enter their house.

Jimmy could visit Libby at her old age home by himself, but this he did only rarely. He was always working, and his wife wanted him at home.

It wasn't long before Libby's heart began to fail. She went in for open heart surgery, and she never came out. She never awakened from the anesthesia. They did this surgery to everyone now and acted as if there was nothing to it, but look what happened to Libby—and look at Jack. They weren't going to put Muriel under that knife.

"Mrs. Margolin?" the nurse announced, too loudly, and Muriel stood up, put her shoulders back, and walked through the door to the examining room where she undressed, put on a paper robe, and waited again for the doctor.

She waited another fifteen minutes, and then the examination took less than five. The doctor was grossly overweight. "You're in excellent health. You'll live to 110, Mrs. Margolin," he said, when he was finished.

"Do you think so?" she said. "Heaven help me."

FROM THE clinic she drove to Whole Foods to pick up something for her dinner. After years and years, sixty-four years, in fact, of cooking dinner for Jack—night after night, month after month, year after year—she was through with cooking. And the soup at Whole Foods was really very good, so why should she bother? She liked shopping there; it was a lot more pleasant than the Safeway right outside of Laurel Dell. For one thing, Whole Foods was full of young people. The Safeway right outside of Laurel Dell was full of depressing old people from Laurel Dell, people who couldn't drive anymore and were reduced to taking the shuttle there. The food at this Safeway was all flavorless, old-people food.

Back in her condo unpacking her few items Muriel wondered what she would do with the rest of her day. There was something that was nagging at her—Jack's old hospital bed, which still occupied the study. She hated the sight of it! How was she going to get rid of it? She had met a man named Donald on one of the Laurel Dell outings—she had been trying to go on as many of these as possible, hoping to meet some new people, or at least to fill up the time—and he had mentioned that she might be able to donate it to Children's Hospital, which she was happy to do. She just didn't want to donate it to that hospital that had taken first Trude and then Dick, and finally, Jack.

Was Jack really dead?

After she put her few items in the refrigerator, her yogurts, her apples, her carton of soup, she walked down the hall to Emilio's old room, where she had been sleeping lately because the mattress in there was firmer than the one in her room. Her back had been hurting. Although her doctor had told her that it almost certainly wasn't the case, she was sure that her breast cancer had metastasized, and that it had lodged in her back. For the most part, however, she was able to hold that thought at bay.

The closet doors in Emilio's old room were mirrored, and she looked at herself. Could she really be eighty-six years old? Surely she didn't look eighty-six. Except for her backache, she didn't feel the way she had thought she would feel at this age. She still felt like herself, she had the same emotions and sensations she had always had. She opened her mouth and looked at her teeth. Unlike most people she met these days, she still had her teeth, and recently she had been wearing a bleach tray her new dentist had given her, for an hour every night. Her teeth were now white and gleaming, like pearls, like all the strings of pearls she had in her safety deposit box in the bank. She decided to go into her own bedroom where her answering machine was to see if there were any messages.

There were two—the first was from Daphne, who called her every day. The second was from that man she had met on the

Laurel Dell bus—Donald. He wanted to know if she'd like to go out to dinner.

She had gone out to dinner with him a few times before. They always went Dutch treat—he didn't have any money—and she had to drive, of course. He walked with a cane and was always falling over. These dinners out together weren't dates, of course. Donald was much too ugly for her, but at least it was someone to go out to eat with. It was better than sitting alone in her kitchen eating some soup from Whole Foods heated up in the microwave, looking out at Mt. Diablo. She picked up the phone and called Donald back. "Swell!" she told him. "Anything to get out of this place!"

WHEN THEY got to the restaurant, Muriel ordered a martini, and so did Donald. He's pretty ugly, she thought to herself, as she chewed on her olive. He looks like a turtle. Jack had been a tall, good-looking man, a successful man. She picked at her food. There was enough here for two dinners. The steak was huge and so was the potato. It was delicious, but she wanted to keep her shape. She would ask the waiter to pack up half of it for her to take home for tomorrow's dinner. She remembered a time when it was thought shameful to take home leftover food from a restaurant, and if you did, you had to pretend it was for your dog. Everything was so different now. She couldn't believe it.

"Another martini?" the waiter asked, and she nodded and held out her glass.

The waiter probably thought she and Donald were married, an old married couple, and it bothered her that he could jump to this conclusion. "You can bring one for my friend, too," she said, so he would know he was her friend, not her husband, though he wasn't much of a friend, either. Theirs was a relationship of convenience—two old people with nothing in common who needed someone to go to a restaurant with.

SHE WASN'T sure how they got to Donald's condo afterwards. She was driving, of course, though she was still feeling the effects of the martinis. What difference did it make if they crashed and died, anyway? Luckily, they hadn't had to go far. When she pulled up in front of Donald's doorway, he said, "Would you like to come in?"

She wasn't sure why she said yes. She had absolutely no interest in him. He was just a convenience to her, as she was to him.

She found his condo rather small and cramped. Obviously, he didn't have any money. She sat down on his plaid couch and looked around the room. Photographs of his children and grand-children lined the shelves. In the photographs, his children were young and their children were babies. But his children were all middle-aged now, as were hers—God, Daphne was already in her sixties. Her children were already old! What did that make her?

Donald sat next to her on the tacky couch and put his arm around her. He began to stroke her on the shoulders, and then his turtle nose was very close to hers, and he was kissing her. His mouth was wet and cool. Something familiar began to stir inside of her, something she had almost forgotten about entirely. Her numbness melted away, and in its stead, there was this long-for-gotten urgency and excitement. His hands were moving over her sweater in rhythmic motions, and then she woke up as if from a dream and realized what he was up to.

"Are you capable?" she asked him, not knowing where those words were coming from.

"I have a pump," he said.

Revulsion filled her. She pushed him away, leapt up, and ran for the door.

Chapter Five

Flora picked up her mother at the Civic Center BART station in front of the main library, as usual. Muriel loved riding BART and always told Flora about all the old people in Laurel Dell who didn't know how to ride BART, who were afraid to take it, and who, consequently, never came to San Francisco. Many of the old people in Laurel Dell were also afraid to drive, or afraid to drive at night, or were asked to give up driving after smashing into someone else's car in the parking lot of one of the clubhouses.

When Muriel parked in these lots, she told Flora, she was always careful to park her little Mercedes far away from any other cars so no one would crash into her. Although she preferred taking BART to San Francisco rather than driving there, it wasn't because she was afraid to drive. She still drove by herself all the way to Los Angeles, six hours on the desolate truck-ridden I-5 which fed into the Grapevine over the mountains, which led into the twisted morass of freeway interchanges that always reminded Flora of the wires in an electrical box. The fact that her mother regularly took herself on this trip proved to Flora that her mother was stronger than she was and would probably outlive her. In Los Angeles Muriel would visit old friends, play bridge, and see her old dermatologist—a doctor who didn't think that because she was in her eighties she wasn't worth bothering with.

When Muriel took BART to San Francisco she liked to get off at the library so she could check out books. This was the main branch, and it had a better selection than her local branch. Muriel had always frequented libraries. She was a great reader. In the house where Flora grew up, however, there were very few books because her mother always took her books out of the library and then returned them. Flora, consequently, had grown up with a lust to own books, and now she had three floors of her house filled with them. She was an English major in college, and now she was a professor. She needed books.

Muriel came to San Francisco to visit Flora once a week, and they usually went out to lunch at Greens and then to a show at one of the museums or to a movie, or they took a walk at Crissy Field. It amazed Flora that Muriel could walk as long and as far as she could. She was glad for her mother and proud of her, but it also distressed her—shouldn't she, twenty-seven years younger, be a little stronger?

Today, however, they weren't doing any of those things. They were scheduled to visit the Bradshaw House, a retirement residence on Van Ness where each occupant had a small private apartment and there was a communal dining room. Ever since Flora's dad's death and Emilio's departure, Muriel had been telling Flora how she hated eating alone. The Bradshaw House was reputed to be very luxurious, and because she was wealthy and old—the number attached to her age made that clear—she wondered if she shouldn't be living in a place like this, especially since there was an assisted living unit connected to the complex where residents could be moved when the time came.

Flora didn't think this place was suitable for her mother, however. She couldn't imagine Muriel ever needing any assistance. She really didn't understand why her mother was even considering the Bradshaw. Laurel Dell had so much more to offer. Couldn't Muriel see that? In Laurel Dell, Muriel had a beautiful big condominium all to herself, on top of a hill with a view of a mountain. The hills were full of golden grass with huge old wild oak trees in the declivities. Deer, wild turkeys, and quail walked by her window. Ten thousand people lived inside its gates, scattered over the valley and up on the hills. In Laurel Dell Muriel wasn't limited to the society of a hundred or so, as she would be if she moved to the Bradshaw.

"But I don't like eating alone," Muriel continuously protested. "I'm lonely! I don't know what I want to do with my life!"

40

So Flora had made an appointment with the director at the Bradshaw. The facility was only a few years old, and Flora knew its newness appealed to Muriel, who hated old places. Flora, on the other hand, had always loved old houses for their character and charm—her own house was nearly a hundred years old. Perhaps that was why Muriel never cared to spend much time there. "Everything's so different here!" Muriel would marvel when Flora drove them around San Francisco. "In Los Angeles, all the old houses get torn down." And Flora wondered if the reason Muriel never wanted to live in an old house was because she worried that someone might have died there.

Flora drove her car up to the gate of the garage of the building and reached her hand out the window to ring the bell. After she explained who she was and with whom they had an appointment, the gate was raised, and they drove in and parked in a slot marked "Visitor." If Muriel moved here she could park in a slot marked "Resident," or she could give up her car altogether, because there was a limousine driver on call to take residents to the symphony or doctors' appointments or anywhere else they wanted to go. But Flora couldn't imagine her mother giving up her car. Muriel was very proud of her driving and how independent it allowed her to be. Still, eventually she was going to have to give up driving, wasn't she? How old could people be and still drive?

They took the elevator to the lobby. This place was elegant, Flora saw, and everything was oversized, larger than life. The lobby ceiling was several stories high, and there was a large fountain in the center with water cascading. A gleaming black grand piano stood in one corner. Crystal chandeliers hung down; everywhere was polished marble and smoky mirrors, and a hush hung over all. Flora felt like she was in a mausoleum.

They walked over to a desk—it was like the front desk of a hotel—and behind it a man and a woman in smart uniforms stood at computer terminals. "Can I help you?" the woman said, as Flora stepped up.

"This is my mother, Muriel Margolin," Flora said. "She has an appointment at two with the director."

"I'll let her know you're here," the woman said. "Why don't you take a look around while you're waiting? Lunch is just over. You can take a look at the dining room—it's just across the way—if you like."

The double doors to the dining room were enormously tall, oversized, like everything else here at the Bradshaw, and they had huge polished brass door handles. Was this place a mausoleum or was it some idea of heaven? One of the doors opened now as they approached, and a woman Flora knew slightly stepped out. It was Mrs. Katzmeir, one of Jonah's former congregants.

Mrs. Katzmeir's blue-white hair was perfectly coiffed and stiff; she was dressed in a knee-length straight skirt and a silk blouse tied with a bow. Muriel, by contrast, still had mostly brown hair which hung to her shoulders in a soft wave. She was dressed in nice but casual brown pants and a mauve turtleneck. This was how she usually dressed; she hated putting on pantyhose, and she never used hair spray.

"Do you have to dress for dinner here?" Muriel asked Flora.

"Mrs. Rose! Hello! How is the rabbi?" Mrs. Katzmeir said.

"He's just fine, thank you," Flora said. "My mother here, Muriel Margolin, is thinking of moving to the Bradshaw. How do you like living here?" Flora asked her. She didn't introduce her mother to Mrs. Katzmeir because she couldn't remember Mrs. Katzmeir's first name.

"I absolutely love it!" Mrs. Katzmeir said. "I highly recommend it!"

Another woman, a younger woman, had appeared behind them. "Mrs. Margolin?" she asked. She had a strong accent—South African? "I'm the director here, Norma Flynn—how do you do?"

"I highly recommend it," Mrs. Katzmeir—was her name even Katzmeir?—said again, and then she glided away across the polished marble floor in her sensible but clearly expensive shoes. Ms. Flynn had addressed Flora, assuming she was Mrs. Margolin, the elder inquiring about residency.

"I was wondering, is it necessary to dress up for every meal here?" Muriel asked.

"Oh, not every meal," Norma Flynn said. "No, of course not. Women occasionally come to dinner in slacks! Have you seen the dining room yet? We're quite proud of it. I think you're going to be quite impressed." She opened one of the outsized doors, and they peered in.

The chandeliers were enormous. The tables were spread with white linen cloths and set with silver and crystal. "But what if it's cliquey? What if you don't have anyone to eat with?" Flora whispered to Muriel.

"Our chef is world-class. And you're allowed to bring two guests a month for a meal . . ." Ms. Flynn was going on.

"What if you get tired of the food?" Flora whispered to Muriel. She didn't want her mother to move here. Her youthful pretty mother did not belong here in this crypt. Why was her mother so afraid? She might never need assisted living, anyway. Not everyone did. And Emilio had promised if she did he would come back and live with her.

After they had seen the dining room, Norma Flynn took them to see one of the apartments. Unlike the lobby of the building, it was not on a grand scale. In fact, it was quite small. Flora couldn't imagine her mother reduced to living in such a small space. Why, oh why did she think she needed to do this? Because *her* mother, Flora's grandmother had?

"You say there's bridge here?" Muriel asked the director.

"Yes, it's on the top floor. There's a game going on right now! But first I want to show you the beauty parlor," Ms. Flynn said, and she took them to another floor, down a hall to a pink windowless room stinking of sulfur, with dryers and sinks and a manicure table.

This reminded Flora of the last time she saw her Aunt Sonja, the last of her father's siblings, who died shortly before he did. Sonja was the aunt who babysat Flora and Daphne when their parents went out. She was always sweet and always cheerful. She was a plain person, a poor person who had never married. She spent her last months in a nursing home in Santa Monica. Jonah and Flora came to see her on Super Bowl Sunday and found all the residents lined up in front of a big TV in the recreation room. Flora wasn't sure Sonja knew who she was. "I'm Flora, your brother Jack's daughter," she said, and bent down and kissed Sonja's whiskery face.

"He fell down. He fell down and hit his head," Sonja said, smiling. Flora didn't know what she was referring to. Had someone in the nursing home fallen down recently? Or was Sonja talking about her brother Jack, Flora's father? Flora had heard many stories about how her father used to roller skate with his sisters when he was a child in Venice Beach, and how he fell down and hit his head once and went unconscious.

A lady in a wheelchair across the room waved at Flora, and she waved back. Then Flora took Sonja's hand and held it. Her aunt's nails were polished a bright pink. The aides must have done this, Flora thought. Aunt Sonja was too out of it to tell them she never bothered with or cared for such frivolities. Flora had never seen polish on Sonja's nails before now, and the nail polish made Flora sad. It was as if Sonja's real identity were being polished over.

Sonja and Muriel had never liked each other. Sonja had told Flora that her mother didn't realize that life was every day. Muriel was always busy making plans for the future. Now Flora wondered if that weren't a survival mechanism on her mother's part. Muriel gave up living in the present in order to live in the future, in the only way the future could ever be experienced. In this way, she continued to stay alive beyond the present.

Sonja's nursing home was not un-cheerful, even though it was for indigents. In fact, Flora found it a lot more cheerful than the Bradshaw House with all its formality and grandeur. But all this formality and grandeur could not insulate its occupants from the inevitable.

"Here we are—the top floor. This is where our little bridge game is," the director said, as they entered a room done up with Louis Quatorze furnishings. And she gestured toward the gilded card table where four blue-grey coifed matrons wearing expensive knit suits and heavy gold jewelry sat holding cards with fingers ending in bright pink nails. "It's a friendly game," she assured Muriel, not knowing, of course, that Muriel had no interest in a friendly game. That would hardly be a challenge for her.

"Shall we go to my office where we can talk?" Ms. Flynn lilted. And they went back down the elevator to her office where she sat down across the desk from them and handed them brochures.

"A medical exam is required before we accept you," she said, "and of course, we don't admit anyone older than eight-two." She smiled. Muriel was eighty-six, but neither she nor Flora said anything.

"I can tell by your accent that you're not from here," Muriel said.

Where was she going with this?

"No, actually I'm from South Africa," Ms. Flynn said.

"I used to know someone from South Africa. Just a friend," Muriel said. "Nothing more. But he's dead now."

Flora's heart stopped. Years ago, rumor had it, something had happened between her mother and one of her bridge partners, a man from South Africa. Her father had been very jealous, though Muriel had protested her innocence. She and her mother had never discussed it. She thought that her mother had a right to her secrets, that perhaps there were things about one's parents' marriage that they shouldn't have to reveal to their children.

Her mother had been a good wife. She had taken care of her father to the end. But it couldn't always have been easy being married to him. And after his heart attack they might have been afraid to be intimate. They slept in separate beds, but that was because her father wanted a soft mattress and her mother wanted a hard one, she thought, or it was because twin beds were the style then. Flora had never questioned it. But she wondered if it was a burden for her mother to carry the secrets of her married life around with her. She wondered if her mother had been taking this opportunity to reassure Flora in some way. Or perhaps it was simply an instance of the past erupting into the present like a salmon leaping from the vast sea briefly into the sky, because the past never really disappeared, it continued to exist just under the surface.

"WHAT DID you think?" she asked her mother as she was driving her back to the BART station.

"The bridge they play there isn't very good," Muriel answered, then added the refrain: "What am I going to do with my life? I just don't know what to do with my life!"

When Flora had pulled up in front of the library, Muriel added, "But thank you for taking me. I just thought that if I lived in San Francisco I would be less of a burden. I don't want to be a burden to you. My mother was such a burden to me!"

"Mom, you're not a burden to me!" Flora said. "If it weren't for you, I'd never see half the shows at the museums or half the movies. I love our days together!"

It was true, but it hadn't always been so—not because her mother was a burden to her, but because her mother made her angry when she told her to stand up straight and suggested she only eat half a sandwich so she would look better in her clothes; and because often after spending time with her mother Flora felt ugly, inadequate, and inferior; and because her mother had always seemed to favor her sister over her.

But that wasn't happening so much any more. Now she wasn't coming home from an afternoon with her mother feeling angry so much as sad. To her surprise, this new sorrow Flora was feeling was almost harder to bear than the anger. Perhaps this sadness had been lurking under the anger all along, she thought, as she pulled away from the curb, watching her mother disappear down the escalator to the train in her rearview mirror. Then Flora realized she was afraid, not only of her own rapidly approaching expiration date, but of what she had been scared of for her entire life—the phone call that would come when she least expected it, announcing that her name had summarily and irrevocably been changed to *Orphan*, telling her that she could no longer be called *Daughter*.

46

Chapter Six

Muriel's mother was going off with a bunch of strangers. How could she choose to go with them, people she didn't even know, leaving her only daughter behind? Sadie was boarding a bus, without looking back. Muriel stood frozen, helpless, watching her go.

She awoke sobbing, in a strange bed, drenched in her salty tears. It had been a dream. Her mother had been dead for years. Muriel was in her granddaughter's old bedroom, in her daughter Daphne's house, in Portland, Oregon. Daphne came rushing in, wearing her nightshirt. "Mom, what's wrong?" she asked, reaching to hug her.

"It's nothing. It was just a dream," Muriel said, holding her daughter at bay. She would not let her daughter embrace her. It was the role of the mother to comfort the daughter, not the other way around.

Muriel was still the stronger of the two; she was not yet in her dotage, her second childhood. Muriel still had all her marbles, thanks to bridge. It was bridge she was convinced which was keeping her mind sharp. She wished her daughters would learn to play, but neither one had ever shown the slightest interest in learning how. They seemed to think it was a waste of time, but she wondered if either of them had the brains for it. She had flown up yesterday, and today she and Daphne were going to drive to the coast where the tournament was being held at a nice resort. Daphne would read and walk on the beach, and Muriel would play. She was hoping her game would be good. She had already arranged for a partner, Fred, a man she met at a tournament in Colorado a few years ago.

Of course, Muriel would take walks on the beach, too. She wanted to keep her shape so she would look good in her clothes.

It was so much easier to shop for clothes when you were slim. She wished Daphne would lose just a few pounds, but she wasn't going to say anything. Daphne was so sensitive. She always thought Muriel was criticizing her, when all she ever tried to do was give her some good advice, because she was her mother, because she loved her.

Muriel was glad to be away from Walnut Creek, if just for a few days. Everywhere she went there—Macy's, the movies, the restaurants, and especially her condo—reminded her of when she had been at these places with Jack and Emilio. There were too many memories. She couldn't take it. She wanted to move.

"Do you have any coffee?" Muriel asked Daphne. "Let's just have some coffee, then we can get on the road."

"How about some oatmeal, too?" Daphne said. "I don't like to go without breakfast."

It wasn't easy for Muriel to hold her tongue while Daphne drove them to the beach in the new Honda she had bought for herself. She didn't know why Daphne had chosen such a big model. She would have gotten a smaller one, but Muriel had held her tongue. She also thought Daphne could drive a little faster. They were never going to get there. Jack had always driven very slowly and cautiously. In fact, he had once been given a ticket for driving too slowly on the freeway. She had sometimes wished she could have been married to a better driver, but Jack was a good man, a decent man, a faithful man—except that he had up and died on her.

"Do you know where you're going?" she asked Daphne.

"I am just following the directions we got on Mapquest," Daphne said. "Would you like to drive?"

"No, no—you're doing a wonderful job of driving," Muriel said, though it wasn't true.

When they arrived at the inn they found the room quite comfortable, deluxe, and reasonable. They were getting the bridge rate, only paying half of what they would have paid had Muriel not been a bridge player. She still wished Daphne would learn to play, but Daphne turned up her nose at it. She opened the shutters. The room had a little deck, overlooking the water. She slid back the door and stepped out.

Someone was running back and forth on a spit of land by the water, and in the sky above, there was a white thing, hovering.

"What's that?" Muriel asked as Daphne came out on the deck beside her.

"I don't know. A kite, maybe?" Daphne said.

"It's not like any kite I've ever seen before," Muriel said.

"Do you want to get some lunch?" Daphne asked.

"Didn't we just have breakfast?" Muriel asked.

"Mom, that was five hours ago," Daphne said.

"I guess I could eat half a sandwich," Muriel said. She was trying to model for Daphne the idea that you didn't need to eat a whole sandwich for lunch. "Would you like to share a sandwich?"

"Mom, I'm hungry after driving all the way here. I'd like to have a whole sandwich. You can have half a sandwich if you want, though. Maybe they'll sell you half a sandwich."

"I just want to look good in my clothes," Muriel said.

"Mom, you do look good in your clothes," Daphne said.

"Then after lunch, we could take a walk on the beach," Muriel said. "I found out the tournament doesn't start until tonight."

DAPHNE AND Muriel started walking down the beach together, but after they had been going for a while, Daphne said she was going to walk ahead. She wanted to get some real exercise. She needed to walk faster and farther than Muriel, so that was what she was going to do. Muriel could just go at her own pace and turn around when she wanted to. She would meet Muriel back in the room.

Let her go, Muriel thought. She's trying to make me feel old by saying I can't walk as far or as fast as she can. She's trying to show off how young and spry she is compared to me. But I bet I can walk just as far and as fast as she can. Then Muriel remembered the orderlies pushing Jack through the halls of the hospital before his open heart surgery, and their granddaughter Posey doing cartwheels down the hall in front of them. "Show off," Jack had said, making her smile in the midst of her terror, her fear that Jack was about to leave her.

But he hadn't left her then. He had come back after the operation, just not all the way back, and then gradually he had started to recede, to diminish, to disappear. At first she thought he would learn to walk again with physical therapy, but he couldn't. He contracted, and every day, for months and years, he had contracted a little more, until he was gone. A little smile appeared on his face when Muriel walked in the room, but all along he was slowly leaving her, and now he was gone. But where was he—where had he gone?

The waves swirled up almost touching Muriel's sneakers as she made her way briskly down the strand, her shoulders back, her head high. The sea was dazzling, yet somber and churning. The water swirled and rolled out at her feet, each small wave laced with white foam; and then the sea retreated with a *sisssss*, and then there was a roaring sound and a booming. Little birds darted ahead of her on stick-like legs, and the water swirled up before her once again.

She had always loved the beach. When she was young she and her friends used to have bonfires there, and now most of those friends were gone. Where had they gone? The same waves still swirled at her feet. Why was she living so long? What was it for? But she didn't want to die. The waves rolled in, and each one was different, each one new, a delight, a constant delight. Then the waves retreated, and new ones formed a pattern at her feet. She just wanted to see a few more waves unfolding before her. Each one was so exquisite, so new. Up above in the sky she saw the kite again, fluttering and swooping. It seemed to be heading in her direction.

She came to a place where a stream was running into the ocean, cutting a shallow bank in the sand. If she wanted to keep going, she would have to cross over, but she didn't want to get her shoes wet. Daphne had disappeared far ahead of her, way down the beach, power walking, showing off. Muriel walked a few feet up from the water, looking for a place to cross the stream. It was narrower up here. She put up one foot to step across when she happened to look up.

There was something huge hovering above her, a gigantic wave. It had come out of nowhere. Time stopped, space opened up, and she had all the time and space in the world to review her past. She felt no anxiety, but rather, a profound acceptance. She did not look behind her. The bus was loading, and she waited patiently in the line to board. And then the wave came crashing down upon her, and it began dragging her into the sea.

Chapter Seven

Flora couldn't understand what her sister was saying. She was calling from the Oregon coast. Flora knew Daphne was to drive their mother to a bridge tournament there. "What do mean, you think she'll be okay? What happened?" Flora shouted into the phone.

"Well, Mom and I were walking on the beach. And I walked ahead. I have to get my ten thousand steps, you know, and—"

"You left her alone walking down the beach?"

"She was perfectly safe. There's nothing you can do about a rogue wave. I couldn't have done anything if I was walking next to her—"

"What do you mean, 'rogue wave'?" Flora asked. She knew what a rogue wave was, but what did that have to do with their mother? A rogue wave was a wave that, without any warning, rose up out of the sea, reached up, and grabbed people. Every year a few people were dragged to their deaths by them. They could reach enormously high and snatch people from the tops of cliffs.

"You know, a sneaker wave. They come out of nowhere."

"Are you trying to tell me that a sneaker wave got Mom?"

"She was walking along the beach, and she came to a stream, so she had to go back a little from the shore to cross it, and if she hadn't—"

"So the sneaker wave missed her?"

"No, it got her. Just let me explain. It knocked her down and started dragging her into the ocean. But then she managed to stand up—if she had been even a few feet closer to the shore she would have been a goner."

"Did you see this?"

"No, I was too far up the beach. I had no idea until I got back to the room and found her in the bath. Somehow she managed to stand up. I don't know how. She was all wet, but she marched back to the room, and now she's in the bath."

"Promise me you won't leave her alone on the beach anymore."

"It wasn't my fault. But I'll promise, if it makes you feel any better."

"I hope she doesn't get hypothermia."

"I think she'll be okay."

Flora went to visit her mother the day after she returned to Walnut Creek. Muriel would be home only briefly between trips. It took Flora forty-five minutes to reach the gates of Laurel Dell from San Francisco. Her mother had said she might be getting a manicure and a pedicure in the morning, but she was sure she would be back by the time Flora arrived. After she was allowed through by the guards, Flora drove past the golf course, where a white-haired couple were walking their schnauzer; and then, at the other end of the valley, she turned up the hill and climbed until she came to her mother's house. There she got out of the car, walked up the path, and rang the bell.

No one answered.

Muriel had once given her a key, but Flora didn't know where she put it. Her mother was probably still at the nail salon. She went back to the car to wait.

Between the curb and the sidewalk in front of Muriel's house there was a thick carpet of lawn. The street was extremely silent and the sun poured down. Birds hopped here and there. Muriel still didn't come. Somehow this scene spread before her reminded Flora of her childhood—the lawn, the silence, the sun, the waiting, the worry about where her mother was. Muriel was probably getting a pedicure, but she could be dead inside the house—of a stroke or an overdose. If she didn't come within a half hour, Flora would call security and have them open the door for her.

Then finally, after twenty minutes, Muriel pulled up in her little Mercedes.

"Didn't I tell you I was getting a pedicure?" she asked Flora, when they were inside, sitting at the kitchen table. "Would you like something to eat?" she asked. "We could split a yogurt."

"That's okay," Flora said. She rarely felt hungry when was with her mother. Being with Muriel reminded her that she didn't really need to eat as much as she ordinarily thought she did. The presence of her mother allowed her appetite to be completely under her control, as it seldom was otherwise. It was as if her mother's presence gave her special powers. She noticed that there was a jewelry box on the kitchen table next to a pile of newspapers.

"I was just at the bank to take some jewelry out to take on my trip," Muriel explained. "My bag's all packed. When I was there, I saw my three watches. One was Grandma's—do you remember it? It's pink gold, with rubies and diamonds."

Flora did remember it. When she was a child, she thought it was the most beautiful thing she had ever seen. The design was from the twenties, Flora realized now, but when she was a child she didn't think of decades or fashions which had passed. This watch was eternally beautiful to her.

"Then there was my diamond watch, the one Dad got for me for our twentieth anniversary."

How Flora used to love *that* diamond watch. It was so beautiful and delicate. It must have been from the fifties, she thought, now. How she used to dream of having something so pretty when she grew up.

"And the third one was the gold watch with the little face encircled by little diamonds that I got for myself. Do you remember that one?"

Flora did remember. That one was from the seventies, the time of Flora's coming of age, a long time ago.

"Can you imagine having to wind a watch? Can you imagine a watch that ticks?" Muriel said. "I can't believe how old I am! When I die, those watches will belong to you and your sister."

Flora thought of the ticking of the clock in the Cosmic Court-room, and how the hands of the big clock on the wall were going around and around. "Only if you die before I do," she said.

"Of course I will," Muriel said. "I just want to finish going through the paper for coupons," Muriel said, "then we can go out for a little walk. Look at this." She folded the paper back and handed it to Flora.

It was an article about a man who had been released from prison after seventeen years of being incarcerated for a crime he didn't commit. A young female detective had taken on his case. She ordered DNA testing which, when it came back, proved him innocent. The governor was about to sign a check for $150,000 in reparations—the check was on the governor's desk, waiting to be signed. With the money, the freed prisoner planned to buy a brick house in Mississippi. The man, who was mildly retarded, had learned to read in prison, but only well enough to read the Bible. He wasn't bitter about what the state had done to him. He forgave his captors. But on the very day he was released, a black SUV ran him down and killed him. They never found the driver of the SUV.

"Isn't that a weird story?" Muriel said.

"I wonder who the driver was," Flora said. "Maybe it was the Angel of Death coming to collect a soul long overdue. Maybe it was unjust that the man was in prison for seventeen years, but maybe the jail was keeping him safe. Maybe while he was in jail his expiration date couldn't be enforced."

"What?" Muriel asked.

"Never mind," Flora said. She had never told her mother about her own expiration date. Muriel would have thought she was crazy.

"Look at *this* article," she said, handing the paper back to her mother. The bird flu had spread to Europe, where people in protective suits removed dead swans from the water, bending their necks so they would fit into plastic bags, doing their part to try to head off the global pandemic, just as people were doing in Africa and Turkey, where they were throwing the carcasses of birds into a pile, pouring gasoline on top of them and lighting a match, or exterminating thousands of birds in avian death camps, but not because they wanted to do it, because it had to be done. And in a neighboring article the polar ice cap was melting, and polar bears were going extinct.

But her mother didn't seem to care about birds and polar bears. She was only interested in bridge. Tomorrow, Muriel was going to another bridge tournament, this time in Sacramento. Flora found it puzzling that her mother wanted to travel so much. It was as if she were running for her life, as if she thought running would keep her safe, because it was harder to hit a moving target than one who stayed home.

Perhaps Flora should have been running, too. She was the one with the death sentence hanging over her head, after all. But what was the point? There was nothing one could do about a heavenly decree. She was not her mother. Her mother seemed to have a special contract with heaven which stipulated that she would be allowed to live forever if she could run fast enough. She had survived being pulled into the ocean by a rogue wave! She was untouchable.

"I know I've been traveling a lot, but I just don't want to stay home. There are too many memories here. I can't take it."

"But what's wrong with memories, if they're good memories?" Flora asked.

"It's just bridge," Muriel said. "I wouldn't be traveling so much if it weren't for the bridge. It's keeping my brain exercised. It's the bridge that's keeping me from getting Alzheimer's."

Flora didn't say anything, but she didn't agree. Beatrice, her mother-in-law, had been a brilliant woman who had used her brain all the time, and she had gotten Alzheimer's. Flora was of the opinion that Muriel's clarity was just a happy fluke of genetics. To Flora, playing cards was a waste of time. She just didn't see the value of it. A game of cards didn't produce anything.

But, of course, it didn't destroy anything, either. Each game was like a snowflake, following a unique trajectory, and then it melted away, and it was gone. There were red cards and black cards, and there were four suits. Players were paired with partners and sat next to opponents. Then the cards unfolded their secrets, combining and resolving into patterns. Each game was an excursion into a separate universe. Sitting in the four cardinal positions, the players spoke to each other in the language of numbers which combined and recombined in patterns, reaching into the elemental, abstract nature of all things.

Perhaps it was more than just a game, after all.

Chapter Eight

Muriel's trip to the bridge tournament in Sacramento was almost called off. She had arranged to play with Carl, a man she met at the bridge club in Oakland. But just as she was about to reserve a room at the hotel where the tournament was being held, where they were offering rooms to the players at a reduced rate again, Carl called and said he couldn't go. His son had been found wandering in the street by the police and had been taken to the hospital. The boy—actually, he was a man, a middle-aged man—wasn't on drugs, he just never ate; he lived on vitamins. He was dazed and confused when they found him. They were keeping him in the hospital a few days for observation. So Carl didn't think he could go to Sacramento while all this was going on. His wife, also, was something of a problem. She was going blind, and this had made her severely depressed, so she never got out of bed. Muriel said she understood, but she was disappointed.

She had desperately wanted to get away from Laurel Dell and all her memories. At least the people from the Children's Hospital had finally come and taken away Jack's hospital bed. After it was gone, she had given the room a thorough cleaning, and then she rolled the TV on its cart in from the living room, from the place where she used to sit watching programs with Emilio and Jack. Jack's old room would now be the TV room, and the image of sitting on the loveseat in there watching TV could now be laid over the memory of Jack contracted on the mattress, a box of diapers and baby wipes laid out on the dresser standing against the far wall.

Sometimes Muriel fell asleep in here now, watching DVDs she checked out from the Laurel Dell library. She was grateful to Donald for suggesting she call the hospital about the bed. She was also grateful to Donald for recommending his cleaning lady. Muriel did not want to waste her life—whatever was left—cleaning house, the way her mother had.

She had not heard from Donald since the night of the martinis, the night she ran out of his condo. She didn't mind, she didn't miss him. She had found a few other people to go out to eat with, and she assumed he had, too. She wondered if he was still alive, even. She would have to ask their mutual cleaning lady.

She had made a new friend, Pauline—also a recent widow— whom she now relied on to go out to dinner. Pauline loved to dine at good restaurants, but what she loved most was her house. She had completely remodeled and redecorated her condo, and she was very proud of it. Muriel did not like to have Pauline come to her own house, as Pauline was very critical. She thought Muriel should do more to decorate it, should get new carpets and new furniture.

But Muriel wasn't interested in fixing up her house. What was the point? How long could she live? If she got new furniture, she would never live long enough to get her money's worth out of it. But the couch and loveseat in the new TV room did look awfully shabby. Their cat Tabby had seen to that.

Tabby had ruined all their furniture, but they had loved that cat. And Tabby had comforted Muriel, sitting on her lap and purring after Jack died and after Emilio moved out, until the cat had died, too.

It wasn't fair. Was she cursed? For a few moments she had considered getting another cat, then rejected the idea. She wanted to be free to travel, to go to tournaments whenever she wanted. She didn't want to be tied down by a cat. Without one she could now safely buy new furniture. So she began to browse the shops when she was downtown in Walnut Creek doing her errands, and one day she saw a couch that reminded her of the first one she had ever owned, the couch they had purchased for the first house she and Jack had built together, the house in Brentwood. It was a camelback couch. Muriel went back to look at it several times, and then, when the salesman told her they would take her old couch away for free, she bought it.

When they placed it in her living room she stepped back to look. It was higher than the other furniture in that room—the chairs she had brought from Beverly Hills which she had reupholstered as soon as the cat died. Muriel wasn't sure all these pieces from the different eras of her life could really coexist. She didn't love the effect. But what did it matter? She wasn't Pauline. She didn't care about furniture, about decorating, about making a home here. This wasn't her home. She didn't have one. The truth was, the only time she really felt at home was when she was sitting at a card table, holding her hand in front of her, waiting for the bidding to begin.

The other person she had found to go to dinner with was Pierre, a very accomplished person. He had been a physicist, and then he went back to school and became a lawyer. Although he was her age, he still practiced law. When they went out to eat it was always Dutch treat, of course; it was not a date. Muriel did not find him attractive. But he was company, and a night she went to a restaurant with Pierre was a night she didn't have to eat alone.

Other women often tagged along. There were so many more women in Laurel Dell than men, and that depressed Muriel. As soon as a man was widowed here, before his wife was even cold, hordes of women bearing casseroles would show up on his doorstep.

Muriel joined the Computer Club, the Bird Watching Club, and the Mystery Book Club to try to stay busy, and she played bridge every chance she got. The bridge at Laurel Dell wasn't entirely satisfying, however. There were too many gossips there. What was great about playing at tournaments was that, though she often saw people she knew from other tournaments, it was largely impersonal.

When Muriel was a young bride she often had card parties with other women—with ladies, as women were called then— and she would have to prepare an elegant little lunch. She hated making and serving it, having to set the table with silver, crystal and linen, and having to clean this all up afterwards. Playing bridge in tournaments was nothing like that; there were no luncheons. It wasn't about making small talk about the accomplishments of her husband or her children. It was about using her brain. She was very disappointed that Carl had cancelled on her.

Then he called and said he could go, after all, if she still wanted to.

"But your son," she said.

"He's stable," he said.

"Your wife?"

"She'll manage for a few days. Would you like me to drive? I can pick you up."

So Muriel called the hotel in Sacramento to register for the tournament. But when she did, she found all the rooms at the special bridge rate were taken. When she called Carl to tell him, he told her it wasn't a problem. He used to live in Sacramento, and he knew of another hotel not far from the other one where they could stay for the same price as the bridge rate.

So they went. They had separate rooms, of course. Carl was married, and, besides, he had a big red nose. But it was wonderful to have a man drive her to Sacramento in a big shiny car and to and from the hotel where the tournament was. At night, when they came back from playing, he invited her into his room where he had a huge bottle of gin. He gave her a drink, and then another.

She had never seen such a large bottle of gin. Nor had she ever seen a nose on a man this large and this red before. The gin went immediately to her head, and then it spread through her body, and she remembered this feeling, the feeling of the blood in her veins and her heart comfortably ensconced in her chest, of her lungs expanding, and warmth spreading everywhere; and she realized how numb she had been for so long, and she thought how surprising it was that she could still feel delicious sensations from her scalp to her toes, sensations she had thought were over for her.

"Another drink?" Carl asked, proffering the gigantic bottle.

"I better not," Muriel said. She said goodnight and made her way to her own room.

SHE MET up with Carl again at the breakfast buffet downstairs in the morning. Then he drove them both to the other hotel for the morning game. They had a good game that morning. The cards were infinitely fascinating in their permutations; their bidding was excellent, and they came in first, always a thrill. And while they were playing, Carl's son was no longer anything to worry about, nor were Muriel's children; thoughts of Carl's wife and Jack stayed outside the room. It was a ballroom, with crystal chandeliers and table after table of bridge players all focusing on their game, the hands they had been dealt. It was an infinite, timeless place. It was heaven. This was what heaven must be.

Muriel's accountant, an old friend, had died recently, in the midst of a bridge game. His cards were in his hands. The bid was four hearts. He dropped the cards and clutched at his heart. And then he was gone. That was a good way to go, Muriel thought—at the top of your game—before you were too infirm to play, before old age dragged you down.

CARL LET Muriel off in front of her condo. She took her little suitcase out of the backseat and set it down next to her on the curb. Then she leaned back into the car, her tote bag over her arm, to thank Carl and say goodbye.

"Goodbye, Muriel," he said. "I'm really glad we went."

"Me, too," she said. "Now you better get home to your wife." She slammed the car door shut, catching her tote bag in the door. Carl didn't notice, he began to drive away. Her arm was hooked in the straps of the bag, and she couldn't get it out.

She was being dragged down the road by her arm! She was screaming, but he didn't hear her. He sped up, dragging her along.

There was something funny about this, she thought, as she was dragged down the road—or there would be something funny about this if it weren't so macabre. She only wished she'd had time to say goodbye to her children.

Chapter Nine

It seemed to Flora that she hadn't heard from her mother for several days. She didn't talk to Muriel every day—she left that to Daphne. If there was something to worry about, Daphne would know, and she would call Flora. Flora dialed Muriel's number, but all she got was the machine, with her mother's voice enunciating her name very slowly and carefully—"MuriEL MarGOlin"—and then, in the background, Daphne's voice saying, "Where's pound? Press pound."

"Just calling to see how you're doing—if you got back from Sacramento," Flora said to the machine. "I'm going to the airport to pick up Jonah, now. I'll talk to you later. Love you."

Jonah had been gone for almost a week at a conference, and Flora was excited to see him. If there was truth to her expiration date, she didn't have all that much time left to spend with him. He called her several times a day when he was away, which was good—they could keep up with their talking. But she had trouble falling asleep when he was gone. She did not like being alone in the bed.

She dressed carefully and put a little scent behind her ears and on each wrist. She knew they would have sex as soon as they got back to the house. That was their tradition—to make love right before one of them left the other to go on a trip, and to do it again as soon as they were reunited. It was a practice they had derived from the Zohar or the Talmud—one of those—which prescribed it as a way to seal a marriage and protect it. Jonah had told her that in the whole six years he spent studying rabbinic texts when he was at the seminary, this was the only practical thing he had learned.

He had further explained to her that the Talmud was not a rational text. Studying it was more about opening up patterns in the brain than learning any moral lesson. He had shown her how, on a page of the Talmud, there was a text in the middle, and all around it were commentaries written at different times in history. He explained that on each page of the Talmud there was a conversation taking place between commentators who were years, even centuries, apart. Flora found this highly romantic.

"How was the flight?" she asked when they were on their way back from the airport. Jonah's hand was on her knee. He seemed familiar and unfamiliar to her all at once, friendly and excitingly dangerous.

"There were a few weird things that happened," he said. "For one thing, on the last leg, I started to notice that everyone on the plane, including me, was carrying a time bomb."

"What are you talking about?" They were merging onto 280 now.

"All of us have a bomb inside us, on a timer, set to go off, and the clock is counting down. I was watching a man walk up the aisle—he was still relatively young. But after he passed me, I turned and saw there was already grey in his hair, and then I saw he had a bald spot on the back of his head. He was in the process of dying."

"So you're a people watcher?" Flora said, and she moved one lane to the left.

"That's not the half of it," Jonah said. "When I got to the airport this morning they told me my flight was delayed, which meant I wasn't going to make my connection in Chicago."

"That must have freaked you out."

"They told me I could stay overnight in Buffalo and get a flight out in the morning, or I could fly to Chicago and do the same thing there. But I have to give that talk here tomorrow. So then the woman at the gate said, 'I can get you on a flight to D.C. with a connection to S.F. The plane is just about to leave. I'll have them hold it for you.'"

"That was lucky." Flora merged into the "San Francisco only" lane.

"I ran through the airport, all in a lather. But I made it! I arrived in D.C. and ran for the plane to San Francisco. I barely made that one. Finally, I was settling into my seat on the connection to San Francisco thinking, now I can relax. The plane was almost full. I was in the window seat, and no one was in the middle one, luckily, and then a tiny, wrinkled, brown woman in a white sari took the aisle seat."

"She must have been a widow. Widows wear white in India."

"I was really tired and soon fell asleep. When I woke up, a horrible stench was wafting my way. I could tell it was coming from the tiny woman in the white sari. She was asleep, with her forehead resting on the back of the seat in front of her. The smell was overwhelming."

"What did it smell like?"

"Excrement," Jonah said. "Human excrement."

"Shit!" Flora said, taking the 19th Avenue exit. She had once done some research for a report Posey had to do in high school about women's rights in India. It was even worse for a woman to become a widow in India than it was here. They became impoverished and had to live on charity. They were shunned and became non-persons. Well, to some extent, that was true here, too, Flora thought, remembering all her mother's complaints about the way she was treated.

"It was horrible," Jonah said. "I kept thinking I was going to catch the bird flu from her. When the plane finally landed, she rushed out into the aisle, but she didn't get very far. It must have been at least ten minutes before they opened the doors. It was really hot in there, and the stench was unbearable.

"Finally, I got off the plane and started walking through the airport. I couldn't wait to see you! But when I got to the escalator that led down to the baggage claim I saw the little woman was standing in front of the escalator, blocking it. It looked like she had never seen one before and didn't know what to do."

"I guess she didn't know there are bathrooms on planes, either," Flora said, stopping at a red light.

"How was your day?" Jonah asked.

"I just did some errands. I went marketing, so there'd be some food in the house for you. I don't cook when you're not here. I just eat whatever I find in the refrigerator. I ran into three people I knew at the Cal Mart. It was weird."

It wasn't that weird. San Francisco was really a small town. And the Cal Mart was popular—it was like a throwback to a 1950's market with a model train running around a track high on the wall and little carts for kiddies to push. It served the fancy well-dressed women from Pacific Heights who had their groceries delivered. Flora liked it because they carried a lot of organic produce.

"Who did you see?"

"First I saw Peppy." Peppy was one of Jonah's congregants. Her mother had gotten breast cancer at the same time Muriel did, and she and Flora always compared notes. Peppy's mother had had a rougher time of it—she had to have chemotherapy, while Muriel got by with only radiation. Unlike Muriel, also, Peppy's mother didn't get her breast reconstructed afterwards. She hadn't seen the point.

"Her mother's cancer has metastasized to her lungs," Flora told Jonah.

When she heard this, she felt sad for Peppy and her mother, and she wondered why her own mother had been spared. Muriel hadn't even taken the Tamoxifen they had prescribed to prevent a recurrence.

"That's too bad," Jonah said.

No doubt he would call Peppy and her mother soon to offer his support. His pastoral work—attending to the sick, the dying, and the dead—had afforded him the most satisfaction of all his duties as a congregational rabbi, and he felt he had a special talent for it. Flora had heard him tell certain Talmudic stories about death and dying time and again, and she always found them compelling.

He told her about how Moses, on his deathbed, pleaded with God to spare him, saying he was afraid of the sword of the Angel of Death—of the pain itself. When God promises him he will take him personally, Moses still pleads pathetically for his life, saying he will do anything—live on the wrong side of the Jordan, or as a beast of the field or a bird in the sky. But God says, "Now you have only an hour, now you have only a few minutes."

And Jonah always told the story from the Talmud about when Rav Seorim, Raba's brother, is sitting by his deathbed, watching Raba drifting in and out of death, and Raba sits up and says to him, "Please tell the Angel of Death not to torment me." Rav Seorim says "*Me? I* should tell him? I thought *you* were his intimate friend." Raba replies, "Since my *mazel*, my fortune has been handed over to him, he takes no heed of me." Rav Seorim then says, "After you die, show yourself to me in a dream." Raba dies, and shortly after he keeps his word and appears to Rav Seorim in a dream. Rav Seorim immediately asks Raba, "Did it hurt?" And Raba replies, "No, it was like pulling a hair out of a bowl of milk." But then he goes on to say, "But were the Holy One to say to me, 'Go back to the world as you were,' I wouldn't do it. That's how great a burden the fear of death is."

Flora had often wondered if Jonah's work with the dying, his head-on confrontation with death, wasn't to some degree an attempt on his part to immunize himself against his own overwhelming fear of it. More and more, he had told her, he had been feeling the dirt falling on his own grave, and like Moses and the rabbis of the Talmud, he was finding himself begging for life. "Even on the very worst days of my life," he had said recently, calling from some motel room in Buffalo, New York, where he was at a conference, "even on those days when I'm depressed and exhausted with the TV blaring mindlessly on the other side of the room—I feel how even these days are infinitely rich and infinitely precious, and I pray to God not to take them away."

THE LIGHT was green. Flora continued her narrative of her encounters at the Cal Mart.

"Then I saw Linda. She had her mother with her. Her mother's completely out of it and has a humpback." One thing Flora was sure of, her own mother would never have a humpback. She'd shoot herself first. And she didn't think her mother would ever lose her marbles, either.

"That's a pity," Jonah said.

What was really a pity was the way Jonah's mother had lost *her* marbles. After Norman died, she rapidly began to deteriorate. She was still relatively young, only about sixty-three—and still beautiful—but it was as if her life were over. She never had another relationship, she retreated from the world, and then, when she was seventy, her children had her checked out, and though the diagnosis wasn't definitive, it was pretty obvious that she had Alzheimer's. The disease took fourteen years to run its course.

"And then I saw Evelyn," Flora continued. Evelyn was another congregant. "She's going crazy. Both her husband and her mother seem to be dying at the same time."

"Her husband's quite a bit older than she is, right?"

"He's my mother's age. I think he had his stroke about four years ago, now. He's been totally incapacitated ever since. She's had to have round-the-clock caregivers. And Evelyn's mother's also been on her last legs."

"I didn't know," Jonah said. "I'll have to give her a call."

"You know what Evelyn said to me? She said she feels like her life is over."

"Well, she may feel differently once they're both dead."

"Maybe. I told her, you never know what's going to happen next. She shouldn't just give up on life! She seemed so sad. But she did get very excited when she saw the Brussels sprouts."

Thinking of these three women and their three mothers had made Flora feel sad herself. All three had reversed roles with their mothers. They were taking care of them. Mothers were supposed to be the ones who took care of their children, who lifted Volkswagens off of them with their bare hands when they were pinned underneath. Flora knew she was lucky to have a mother who, although perhaps not particularly inclined to be lifting compact cars off her daughters, nonetheless didn't need any caretaking herself.

"I think Brussels sprouts are very exciting," Jonah said, and he slid his hand up Flora's leg.

They had arrived at the house. Flora pulled into the driveway, they unloaded the luggage, and she helped Jonah carry it all up the stairs. She had put fresh flowers in their room. The Cal Mart always had a wonderful selection of them. Jonah began to get undressed.

"Are you tired?" she asked.

"Not too tired," he said. "Why don't you get undressed and get in bed?"

So she did.

FLORA COULD not imagine anything more wonderful than love-making with Jonah. Each time they did it, she was amazed afresh by how spectacular it was. It was like being inside a rhapsody, she thought. It was as if they were constellations—as if he were constellating her, and together they were flying through the stars. She felt this lovemaking was some sort of heavenly gift which she didn't deserve, but without which she couldn't live. If too many days passed between their couplings, Flora would feel herself losing touch with reality. Nothing would have any substance for her; she would feel out of joint with the universe. She wondered how single people got by, how they retained any sense of proportion about anything, any sense of belonging to the whole of existence. But probably not everyone was like her. Probably many single people had lives just as meaningful and fulfilled as hers. Perhaps they even experienced their lives in a deeper way than she did, since all her experience was buffered by being with Jonah. This was just the way she was constituted—she was a person able to be only half alive without the one she loved.

Perhaps that's how Beatrice had been constituted. Poor Beatrice! If only she had been able to live out her life with her beloved Norman. But he had died on her. Flora didn't know what she would do if anything happened to Jonah. All she could imagine was sitting on a folding chair at the side of his grave conversing with him all day.

Jonah, luckily, seemed to feel the same way about her. A lot of men his age had mid-life crises. They became terrified of getting old, of dying, and they left their long-time spouses, the mothers of their children, and married young wives. Did spending their time with someone so much younger than they were make them feel like they were younger, too? It could also make them feel older, she thought, having to explain who the Beatles were, and all that. Jonah claimed that he found young women totally unappealing, that they were like another species to him. Flora was fairly certain Jonah would never leave her for a younger one. Even though she herself was no longer as supple and smooth as she used to be, Jonah still seemed to think her beautiful.

Recently, she had been making peace with her body. When she was younger, she was always wishing her body was more this way or less that way. She had wasted a lot of time wishing herself otherwise. Lately, however, she had come to appreciate her body. It had served her well, and it continued to be a repository of pleasure for her. If Jonah could love her body, then so could she.

They often had conversations about what they would do if they lost their bodies, or significant parts of them. "If you lost all your arms and legs, if you were just a brain, I would keep you in a jar on the side of the bed and I would still love you," they would reassure each other.

"I don't want to, but I have to get up and work on my talk for tomorrow," Jonah said, giving her one last hug. He pushed back the covers and stood up, looking for his underpants.

Flora sat up in bed. "What's your talk on?"

"It's about Rabbi Akiba."

"What about Rabbi Akiba?"

"I'm going to tell some stories from the Talmud about him."

"Tell me one," Flora said.

"Okay, I'll tell you just one." He pulled on his shorts and crawled back under the covers.

"This is the story about his daughter. When she was born, the astrologers prophesied that she would be bitten by a poisonous snake and die on the day she was brought to the wedding canopy.

"Now flash forward to her wedding day. That's how the Talmud tells a story. It's very economical. Rabbi Akiba's daughter wakes up in her maiden bedchamber on her wedding day and reaches over to pull her hairpin from the wall, where she had stuck it the night before. To her surprise, when she pulls it out, there's a snake on the end of it, an asp, a very poisonous snake. Then her father comes running into her bedchamber and says 'What did you do? What did you do?'

"He means, what did you do to avert the evil decree? The evil decree was that judgment that came down from Heaven proclaiming that she should die on the day of her wedding. The snake was waiting in the wall to bite her and make the prediction come true, to carry out her sentence. But without being aware of it, she had impaled it with her pin before it could bite her. When Rabbi Akiba asks what she has done, he means, what good deed has she done to avert this fate? Because, as it says in the Talmud, everything is foretold and there is free will—our fates are predetermined, but, nonetheless, there are certain things we can do to avert an evil decree: acts of charity, prayer, repentance, changing your name—"

"I know about that one," Flora said.

"So Rabbi Akiba wants to know what his daughter did. 'I didn't do anything,' she says. 'But when everyone was feasting at my rehearsal dinner last night, I happened to hear someone knocking at the door. No one else heard, so I went and answered it. Standing at the door was a poor beggar. He was starving to death, so I loaded a plate from the sideboard and brought it to him.'"

"That's a great story. I wonder if I can do anything to avert my evil decree," Flora said.

"You don't have an evil decree," Jonah said, getting out of bed and putting on his pants.

AFTER HE had gone into his study, Flora decided to try her mother again. This time Muriel answered.

"How are you?" Flora said.

"I think I'm okay. I think I'm going to be okay," Muriel said.

"What do you mean you think you're going to be okay?"

"I don't think I broke anything when I was dragged by the car."

"What you do mean when you were dragged by the car?" Flora asked.

So Muriel told her the whole story—how the car was dragging her, and how the straps of the tote bag finally broke, setting her free, and how her friend just drove away never looking back and probably didn't even know it had happened. "I'm pretty black and blue," she told Flora. "But I don't think anything's broken."

"Are you sure?" Flora asked.

"Yes," Muriel said. "I went to the Laurel Dell clinic, and they checked me out. Of course, the doctors are pretty terrible there. They don't know anything. If they did, they wouldn't be bothering with old people. I'm just black and blue—but it's already getting better. I'm starting to turn green."

"The Angel of Death has been after my mother again," Flora said, when Jonah walked back into the bedroom.

"What are you talking about?" he asked her.

So she told him. "So there must be an evil decree out on my mother," she concluded.

"Of course there is," Jonah said. "There's one out on each of us." He reached for a book from the shelf and started leafing through the pages. Finally, when he found what he was looking for, he said, "This is what it says in the Talmud." And he read her this passage:

> Everything is a loan against a pledge;
> a net is spread over all the living.
> The shop is open, the shopkeeper extends credit,
> The ledger is open, the hand records,
> whoever would borrow may do so;
> the collectors make their rounds daily,

they exact payment from everyone,
with or without consent;
they have a reliable record.
The verdict is a just one,
and everything is ready
for the final accounting.

Chapter Ten

It took several weeks for all of Muriel's bruises to go away. She just wore sunglasses and makeup while she was healing and went about her business. She didn't hide in her house—she would have gone crazy if she had to stay home. She still went to the Bridge Club, she just played in her sunglasses. That wasn't as bad as some people. She frequently saw people at the Bridge Club or at tournaments with oxygen canisters. It was becoming more and more common. She healed quickly and had only the slightest trace of green left around her eyes when she left for the tournament in Colorado.

She had been looking forward to this for some time. Fred had invited her to stay with him. He lived not far from the hotel where the tournament was being held. It was really nice of him. And, of course, it was all on the up and up, she assured Flora and Daphne. She had her own room and her own bathroom at his place. He was much too young for her—he was sixty-five—she was thinking about fixing him up with Daphne, in fact. She had no idea if he'd be interested. She knew he had never been married, but little else about him. They never talked about anything personal. All they talked about was bridge. It was better that way. And she knew she'd be perfectly safe staying at his house because he knew how old she was.

He had told her. He had looked her up on the Internet. Though she didn't let on to him, this had made Muriel extremely angry. It was horrifying to her that anyone could just go to the Internet and find out how old she was.

Although his condo was very comfortable, there was one weird thing that happened the last time she stayed with him. After she was in bed at night, she heard him walking outside her door.

Then she smelled an intense, sharp smell. It smelled like rubbing alcohol. And then she heard his footsteps walking away. She thought of saying something about it in the morning, but decided not to, in the end.

This time she wasn't the only bridge player who would be staying at Fred's house. Justine would be staying there, too, a woman who had a crush on him, Muriel happened to know. Muriel didn't mind. She wasn't interested in Fred. Justine was more his age. She was a widow, too. Her husband had gone spelunking one day, and he had gone into a cave and never come out. Muriel didn't think Justine had a chance with Fred, however. She was too big. She had too big an appetite. When they went out to eat, she ate everything on her plate.

Muriel enjoyed playing with Fred, but Justine wanted to play with him, so Muriel said she'd try to find another partner when they got to the hotel. As they walked in the door, Fred saw someone he knew and went over to talk with him. In a few minutes, he came back with this fellow trailing behind him—a tall, white-haired old man wearing a jumpsuit.

"This is Wilbur," Fred said. "He's looking for a partner, too, Muriel. He'll play with you."

Muriel and Wilbur chatted for a few minutes. By coincidence, his wife had died around the same time Jack had. They went in to play and it turned out that Wilbur was a pretty good player, for an old guy. They won.

When Muriel met up with Fred and Justine at the end of the day she found out they hadn't done so well. Here Muriel had been mad that Justine had gotten to play with Fred, and Muriel had done better. "Ha!" Muriel thought. They decided to go out to eat, to a restaurant they liked, one they had been to before, and, to their surprise, the host recognized them. "Here are my favorite patrons!" he said, and showed them to the best booth in the dining room. It was flattering and gratifying to be recognized like this. They all ordered martinis.

The dinner was much too big for Muriel, of course, but she didn't ask for a doggie bag, because they weren't going back to

Fred's before the evening game. Justine cleaned her plate. She wasn't going to get anywhere with Fred if she didn't start watching what she ate. But Muriel didn't say anything.

She was feeling pretty good, and still a little tipsy from her cocktail, when they walked back into the hotel lobby. Sitting there on a big round hassock was Wilbur, the old man she'd had such a good game with. He looked forlorn. Apparently, he had no one to go out to dinner with. Or maybe he couldn't afford to go anywhere nice. "Oh here's my boyfriend," she said, sitting down next to him and touching his leg.

She was just joking, but he didn't seem to know it.

"Why don't we go down to the parking garage and sit in my car?" he asked her.

She wasn't going to do that, of course. She didn't know him from Adam.

So they sat together on the hassock and talked. He had been a career officer in the Air Force. That was a coincidence, since Jack had been in the Air Force during the war, too—but, unlike Wilbur, Jack had never left the ground.

"I flew many missions in Vietnam," Wilbur told her.

This intimacy made Muriel feel two strong conflicting emotions at once. The first was tremendous admiration for Wilbur for being able to fly a plane. Jack had barely been able to drive a car. He drove so slowly that it drove Muriel crazy. Wilbur was obviously tremendously brave. His bravery was enjoyable to her.

The other emotion she felt was confusion, changing to chagrin. If Wilbur was in the Vietnam War, then, despite appearances, he must be quite a bit younger than she was. It was a good thing she hadn't mentioned that her husband had been in the Air Force in World War II. She didn't want him to dismiss her as just an old lady. Even she thought of old people as non-persons.

"How old was your wife when she died?" Muriel asked.

"Sixty-seven. She was four years younger than me. I never thought she would be the first one to go."

Muriel did the math. She was very good at math, even when she was a little bit drunk. His wife had died a year ago. If she was sixty-seven then, Wilbur had been seventy-one. That was a year ago, so Wilbur was now seventy-two, fourteen years younger than she. This was odd, because she had assumed he was older than she was. This was also problematic, because it was clear that as soon as she had said, "Here's my boyfriend!" that he had become her boyfriend. It was as if the words had been magic. She hadn't meant anything by it. She had thought Wilbur was just an old man, no one she would ever be interested in. She was a little drunk, and the words had slipped out. She had only meant them as a teasing joke, and she had no intention of really trying to make Wilbur her boyfriend.

But when she pronounced those words she hadn't known Wilbur was a pilot. The news that he was one seduced her. He was moved from the "old man" peg in her mind to the "manly man" peg. Now she was pleased to have him as her boyfriend.

But how could he be her boyfriend? He was fourteen years younger than she was, though he didn't seem to realize this. She would have to be careful not to tell him how old her children were. Of course, he could look up her age on the Internet, like Fred did. She cursed the Internet. And Fred could tell him how old she was, if he chose to. But why would Fred do this? Only if he knew Wilbur was her boyfriend. She would have to keep this a secret from Fred.

She sat on the hassock a long time with Wilbur. Their conversation soon turned to bridge. It turned out he was as much a fanatic about bridge as she was. In fact, he was inventing a new way of bidding that was going to make him famous in the bridge world. She was very interested in hearing about it. He was going to be doing the bridge circuit around the Southwest in a few weeks, and he was going to be trying out his new system. He was looking for a partner to travel with him.

As it happened, going on the bridge circuit was something that Muriel had always wanted to do, she told him. She had never done it because her absence would have upset Jack if she left him for several months or even weeks. Jack himself had never played. He was always too busy to learn. Jack would have missed her too much if she had gone. Wilbur now asked Muriel if she'd like to go with him through the Southwest, starting in Albuquerque, in two weeks. She said yes.

Just as they were exchanging email addresses, Fred and Justine came up to them. It was time for the evening games to begin. Tonight, Muriel was scheduled to play with Fred. She said nothing to him about what had transpired between her and Wilbur. Their game was so-so. Afterwards, he drove her and Justine back to his condo, and in the morning, he drove them both to the airport.

Chapter Eleven

Flora picked her mother up at the main library. Muriel had an errand to do downtown—she wanted to go to her jeweler's—and then she wanted to go to Greens for lunch and after to Crissy Field for a walk along the bay. Flora always allowed her mother to choose what they would do on their weekly visits. There was no point in suggesting anything to her or countering her wishes, because Flora knew that in the end they would always do what her mother wanted to do. Her mother's will was a lot stronger than hers, and besides, Muriel's ideas usually turned out well. And why not cede the authority to her? After all, she was the mother. She was due respect.

"Do you know where you're going?" Muriel asked Flora as they pulled away from the curb.

"Yes, I live here," Flora said.

"Everything's so different," Muriel said.

"Not to me," Flora said. "We're going to park in the Sutter-Stockton garage. It's just a few blocks from your jeweler. It's a city lot—it won't be too expensive." Flora knew her mother hated to pay for parking. She knew her mother thought parking should be free—that it was a God-given right. "Why do you want to go to the jeweler?" she asked.

"I broke the clasp on my necklace," Muriel said. "I'd like to get it fixed before I go on my trip."

"What trip?" Flora asked.

"Didn't I tell you? I'm going to Albuquerque next week."

"How long will you be gone?"

"I don't know."

"What do you mean, you don't know?"

"Well, I'm meeting up with this man I met in Colorado—Wilbur, I think his name is. We're going to go out on the bridge circuit."

"You're going to be traveling with him?"

"Yes. But he's a nice guy."

"Who is this Wilbur?"

"It's the strangest thing. I thought he was an old man. But he's fourteen years younger than me! If he ever finds out how old I am, he'll run like crazy. He's from Texas and he grew up on a farm. He's a Baptist, I believe. A real Southerner."

"Mom, you're a Jew from Beverly Hills."

"Oh, it's okay. He's not an anti-Semite or anything. He's just a simple farm boy."

"Mom, are you sure he's not after your money?" Flora felt obligated to ask this.

"Yes, I'm sure. He doesn't know how much money I have. So, what do you think? His wife died the same time Dad died. I think he's lonely. All he does is travel around playing bridge. It's just that I've always wanted to go on the bridge circuit."

"I don't know what to think. It sounds like you're going to have an adventure."

"Why shouldn't I?" Muriel asked. "Should I just sit in my condo alone all day?"

"Of course not, Mom. Here we are." Flora parked and led Muriel to the elevator, then out and down a few streets to Muriel's jeweler, who was in the Shreve building.

"I broke the clasp on this necklace," she said to him, when he had opened his little window. "I wear it all the time." She took the necklace out of a little bag inside her purse. It was a gold chain with a diamond in the middle of it. "This was the diamond from my engagement ring," she said.

Flora looked at it. She had seen this necklace on her mother's neck for as long as she could remember. But she hadn't realized that the diamond was from the engagement ring her father gave her mother, the ring she returned to him several times before he finally forced her to keep it.

"No problem," the jeweler said. "I can have it ready for you next Thursday."

"I'm leaving on a trip on Wednesday," Muriel said. "Maybe my daughter can pick it up for me."

"I can do that," Flora said, taking the ticket the jeweler had filled out after dropping the necklace into a small manila envelope. Soon she and Muriel were out on the street again.

"Do you mind if we make a little stop at Gump's?" Muriel asked. "There's something I want to show you there. I was here last week with Pauline. I do things with her sometimes so I don't have to be such a burden to you."

"Mom, you're not a burden to me, but I do have a job. And on Tuesdays and Thursdays I have to be at school all day."

"I know you have a job! I'm so proud of you."

They had arrived at Gump's, and Flora was following Muriel around the store as she peered into the display cases.

"It was here last week. I wonder if they sold it."

"What was here?"

"It was a pin, just like the one Dad gave me, the one that looks like a bee—it's gold with diamonds. Dad always called it 'Burt Bee.' They had one just like it, and they were asking $6,900 for it! Do you know what Dad paid for it? Six hundred dollars! Can you imagine?"

"You can't compare," Flora said. "Things cost more now, but people have more money. Money's not worth as much."

"Where is it? It was here last week. I saw it with Pauline."

"Let's give up, Mom. I believe you." She couldn't understand why it was so important for her mother to show her this pin, or why her mother was so upset she couldn't find it. What did it mean to her? It seemed to excite her that a bauble she'd had for years, which she hadn't seen much value in, had been priced so high. But why did she need to show this to Flora?

Once again, Muriel seemed to be talking to her in code, in a secret language reserved for mothers and daughters. She and Lulu also had a secret language, the language of Ob. You put "ob" after the first letter of each syllable of a word. It was a language that

82

took twice as many syllables to speak as any other, a language other people couldn't understand, and it was a language that made everything funny. Posey had tried to learn it, but she had never become fluent. But Ob was nothing like the secret tongue which Muriel spoke to Flora in. This wasn't a funny babbling, it was a delicate, subtle language. It communicated with the utmost clarity and the least in the way of embarrassment. It spared everyone's feelings, and it allowed all parties to retain their dignity. It was the way Muriel was telling Flora that even if she hadn't valued Flora's father very much at first, she had come to treasure him, enormously. She was telling Flora her father wasn't forgotten—even though she was about to go off on a road trip now with a strange man from Texas, a cracker. She was telling Flora it was all right. She knew what she was doing. And Flora didn't doubt it. There was nothing Flora could do about it, anyway. Her mother always did exactly what she wanted to do.

"So TELL me about Wilbur," Flora said, when they were seated at a window seat at Greens looking out at the bay and the Golden Gate Bridge coming in and out of the fog. Flora always gave Muriel the good seat—the seat facing the bridge—when they came here. After all, Flora lived in San Francisco and saw the bridge all the time. And she had heard Muriel complain more than once that when she went out to eat with Pauline, her friend always raced ahead—though she could barely walk. Because, despite being several years younger than Muriel, her hips and knees hurt her—so she grabbed the best seat for herself, the seat with the view.

"Well, he was a pilot in the Vietnam War," Muriel said.

"That's horrible," Flora said. "He probably killed a bunch of people."

"But don't you think that's brave? To fly a plane?"

"Does he know you have a daughter who spent her youth protesting that war?"

"Of course not! I wouldn't want him to know how old my daughter is."

"If I ever meet him, I'll wear a pinafore and my hair in pigtails."

"Who knows how long this will last? Once he finds out how old I am . . ."

"So have you been talking on the phone?"

"Yes, every day. And he emails at least two times a day."

"Mom, I'm happy for you. You're going to have an adventure."

"I guess you could call it that."

"You're sure he's honorable?"

"Absolutely. He's extremely upright. Very patriotic. Won't buy anything that's not made in America."

"Oh, brother. What does he think about the fact that you drive a Mercedes?"

"He doesn't have to know that."

"He sounds pretty right wing."

"I guess so. But it's not about that. It's about bridge. He's a terrific bridge player. It's a thrill to play with a really good player."

On the day Muriel left for Albuquerque, Daphne called Flora all upset.

"Do you know that ever since Viagra was invented, there's been a high incidence of AIDS among the elderly? Do you think he's after her money?"

"Daphne, calm down. You know you can't stop her from doing whatever she wants to do. It bothers me that he's so right wing, but Lulu said Grandma should have a free ride. At her age, she can do whatever she wants. I have to get off. Someone's trying to call."

The person who was trying to call was Muriel. She had arrived in Albuquerque. She was at the hotel where Wilbur was going to meet her. He had called, he was on his way.

Flora saw her mother there, as in a vision. She was sitting on a high couch in the middle of the hotel lobby, like a little girl on a big piece of furniture, her legs dangling down, waiting for Wilbur to come.

Chapter Twelve

Muriel sat on a high couch. She felt very, very young and innocent. She couldn't exactly remember what Wilbur looked like, and she hoped she would recognize him. She knew he was very tall—at least six-three. They were going to look like Mutt and Jeff together. Would he, being so much younger than she, even know who Mutt and Jeff were? She wasn't really sure, herself. If she had once known, she had forgotten. If Jack were there, she would have been able to ask him. He would have lifted his head briefly and given her the information. Toward the end, although Jack had spoken less and less, she could ask him any sort of arcane question and he always had the answer.

She thought maybe Mutt and Jeff had been cartoon characters. She had read the comics every morning in the *L.A. Times*, after turning the pages slowly and clipping out coupons, sitting at the yellow counter in their kitchen in Beverly Hills, enjoying a glass of the orange juice she had just squeezed, the juice she had squeezed every day for herself and Jack and the girls, when they were still at home. She remembered when there were still orange groves all over Southern California, and the smell of the orange blossoms. It worried her a bit when she forgot things, like who Mutt and Jeff were. Thank goodness for bridge, she thought. If it weren't for bridge, she'd probably be like one of those old people who didn't know what a spoon was for.

"Muriel?"

Wilbur was looming over her. It made her laugh, how tall he was, and that he was wearing a jumpsuit.

"Are you ready to play?"

She was. He took her by the arm and led her into the ballroom.

Wilbur had reserved a room for them at the Motel 6. He insisted upon paying, he was a real gentleman. Of course, it wasn't very much. She gathered that Wilbur didn't have much money, he was living on his pension. His needs were simple. He was a simple person, refreshingly so.

Wilbur unfolded the suitcase stands and set their bags on top of them. Muriel unzipped hers and started to rummage around inside it. She had found out a lot about Wilbur in their email exchanges. She had learned that his wife had been a nurse, but that she had injured her back somewhere along the way lifting a patient; and she had been bedridden the last several years of her life, and that Wilbur had cared for her. She had learned that Wilbur had been born on a farm in the Deep South during the Depression, and that when Wilbur was small his father had died in a farming accident—he had been eaten by a machine. Wilbur's older brother had come running across the field. It was something like that. It had all gotten mixed up in her head with a Faulkner novel Muriel had read when Flora was at Berkeley, and had come home with a suitcase full of books for the summer.

There was another story, which could also have been something out of Faulkner, about Wilbur as a little boy riding on a cart next to his father, who was soon to be dead. Two mules were pulling the cart, and one was refusing to budge. Wilbur's father had a switch with which he was beating the mule who refused to budge, while he was imparting a bit of wisdom to his son which would see him through all the trials and tribulations of the rest of his life: the desperate poverty of Wilbur's childhood on the farm; his time flying a bomber in Vietnam; his experiences flying rich people around the country in private jets after that; his marriage; the birth of his children; his kids' problems, as they grew up, married, and divorced; and finally, his epiphanies at the bridge table. And this advice, simply stated, was, "You have to know which mule to beat, son," which over the years had been reduced to "which mule to beat."

Muriel wasn't exactly sure what it meant, though it seemed somehow proof to her that Wilbur was a man with a good character. She emailed him back asking him what it meant, hoping she didn't sound too dumb, and he emailed back saying, "Somebody has to get beat. Somebody's got to get hurt. But it should be the right person." Muriel still didn't get it, and she had consulted Flora to see what she thought. Flora thought Wilbur was justifying killing people in Vietnam, but Muriel didn't think that was it.

She unzipped her little suitcase and removed her toothbrush. She went into the bathroom. It was perfectly adequate and clean. There was no hair-dryer, but otherwise it was not unlike many other motel bathrooms. She brushed her teeth. They were very white. Bleaching them had taken at least ten years off of her age, maybe more. She wasn't sure if she should get undressed.

When she walked back into the room, still dressed, she found Wilbur had taken off his jumpsuit. He was dressed only in a white tee-shirt and boxer shorts. He reached for Muriel and folded her in his arms.

"It feels good to hug," he said.

"It does," she said. It did.

"I'm afraid that's all I can do. Is that all right with you?"

It would have to be. "Of course," she said.

"Good," he said, and got into the bed. She went back into the bathroom, put on her nightgown, came out, and got into the bed on the other side. He took her into his arms and held her until they were both asleep.

In the morning they went to IHOP for breakfast. She had never been to an IHOP before and couldn't believe how much food they were served and for so little money. He barely spoke, but the silence was not uncomfortable. He was the strong silent type, she decided. Once again, he insisted upon paying. After breakfast, they went back to the motel and checked out. Then he put their suitcases in the trunk of his big heavy Dodge and started to drive toward Las Cruces. As they drove they listened to CDs of country western music which he had brought, music she was totally unfamiliar with, but which she liked, quite a bit. He didn't talk, but she didn't mind. She liked listening to the music and looking out the window at the arid western landscape, and most of all, she liked being driven down the highway by a manly man.

This was the West. Both she and Jack had always loved it. They had both been born in Los Angeles and had gone to Palm Springs for their honeymoon, spending a week horseback riding and hiking to mountain springs. Jack had gone to Glacier Park, hiking and camping with his friends the year before they met. It had been the most wonderful experience of his life. After the girls were born they went on family vacations every summer, visiting every national park in the West. Muriel had never lived on the East Coast, and people who came from there seemed somewhat suspicious to her. It was the West that she believed in, its hot days and cool nights, its endless vistas.

It started to rain. Very soon, the rain was plummeting down upon them, but Wilbur didn't even slow down. He was a terrific driver, and this thrilled her. The rain thrilled her. It was so different from any rain she had ever experienced. It had never rained like this in California. Not with this force. And what did it matter if they crashed and died? She was old enough to die. Yet she knew they weren't going to crash. She had absolute trust in Wilbur's ability to navigate them through the storm, even though he had told her his eyesight had started to fail—that was why he had to stop flying—he was practically blind in one eye.

One of Jack's favorite songs had been "When you walk through a storm, hold your head up high, and don't be afraid . . ." She couldn't remember the rest of the lyrics, but she saw that Jack had been right to believe in the song's message. It was wise. Why couldn't they always have lived by those lyrics? Why had they ever been afraid? What was there to be afraid of? "You'll never walk alone." That was what the song was called, that was what it was about. It was about God, but she didn't think Jack had believed in God. As for her, she didn't know what to believe.

Since it was a question which couldn't be answered, there was no point in asking it. The jury was forever out on that one. Still it felt somehow comforting to think of never walking alone. She was so grateful that, at least for now, she wasn't alone, and she glanced over at Wilbur, his large sausage-like fingers lightly gripping the steering wheel.

Poor Jack, alone in the ground. Well, she would be joining him soon. Soon, just not yet. For now she was with Wilbur, a man she barely knew, and he was driving her through a rainstorm in New Mexico. Wilbur was a real man, solid flesh and blood. The rain sliding down the windshield was real, as was the sound of it pounding on the roof of the car. The sound of the rain on the roof was a deep thrumming which filled the car and all the empty places inside of her

When they got to Las Cruces, they checked into another Motel 6. It was exactly like the last one. Motel 6 was a constant, an eternal stopping place, a bit of eternity, a place where she was able, thank God, to escape the past and all its memories; and equally, a place where the future did not matter, the future didn't exist.

Muriel didn't really believe she had a future with Wilbur. Once he found out how old she was, he would run like anything. What was there for her in the future, anyway? Only disability, what they called "assisted living," and death. The Motel 6, existing outside of time, as it did, was a much better place to be. Looking at the bed-spread, the drapes, and the easy chair prompted Muriel to think how glad she was, also, to be away from the pressure to decorate her condo in Laurel Dell. After purchasing the couch she felt she had exhausted her ability to get herself to decorate. Pauline continued to suggest that she fix up her condo even more, that she hang the paintings she had left leaning against the wall.

Muriel actually intended to hang the picture that had always been in the study in Beverly Hills—a painting of a Joshua tree, a desert landscape. It had been Jack's favorite. She wanted to hang it in the room she had made into a TV room, but she needed to find a handyman. She couldn't hang it herself. But she hadn't had time to look for a handyman. She didn't have time to just sit alone in her condo like Pauline, waiting for one to come.

They unpacked, and while Muriel rinsed out her underpants in the sink and hung them over the shower rail, Wilbur watched TV. It was some right-wing commentator fulminating against liberals. She would never be able to introduce him to Flora. As for Muriel, she did not limit herself to being either on the left or the right. She considered herself an independent.

She was glad she had put a small bottle of Woolite in her suitcase at the last minute, and congratulated herself on having brought with her everything she needed and nothing more. The night before Muriel left to meet up with Wilbur she had gone through her closet to decide what to take, choosing outfits by a strict set of criteria. They had to travel well—they couldn't wrinkle. And they had to be comfortable, containing nothing that was binding or that had a zipper that was hard to pull up. But most important of all, she had to look beautiful in it. Knowing that she would look beautiful in a particular outfit was the determining factor, of course.

Out of everything in her wardrobe, as it happened, there were very few outfits which met all these criteria, so the selection process of what to take was not that difficult. She wondered why she continued to keep clothes which she didn't feel beautiful wearing. Why didn't she just weed out the clothes in her closet and throw everything that wasn't first rate into a bag for the Good Will?

But she had been unable to do that. A voice inside her always protested that she might want these garments in the future—that somehow in the future she might feel beautiful in these garments. And she had argued to herself that she didn't have to be so ruthless with her wardrobe, there was plenty of room in her closet. But now it was a relief to get away from all those outfits in which she felt somewhat less than perfectly beautiful—to have only clothes that she felt flattered her each morning when she got dressed.

Wilbur, for his part, only wore jumpsuits. He had brought along a suitcase stuffed with them, and he put on a fresh one every day. She thought these jumpsuits were ridiculous, but it pleased her that he was so fastidious in changing them.

They had lunch at McDonald's, another place Muriel had never been, and Wilbur paid, again, which she appreciated. It made her feel like she was being taken care of, protected, and that she was being respected the way girls were respected by young men when she was young—when men paid for girls when they went out on dates, and opened doors for them, and kept them on a pedestal.

McDonald's was a wonderful place. Wilbur was introducing her to the whole world of fast food restaurants, a world she had never known, and she found it fascinating. It was just as worthy a world to inhabit as the world of the upscale restaurants she patronized with Pauline and Pierre, back in Walnut Creek. Perhaps it was even a better world, actually, because it wasn't tainted with snobbishness. And the cup of yogurt Muriel ordered was really good—and not too big, either. She finished the whole thing. Then she sat at the table quietly with Wilbur while he nursed his Dr. Pepper and went over the bridge system he had been inventing and perfecting. Finally, he looked up from his scribbling. It was time to drive to the club.

They barely spoke on the way and it suited her fine. This was because they had almost nothing in common except for bridge. There was something quite perfect about this situation. She was with a man, she wasn't lonely, but she was completely independent. Her mind could remain all her own, inviolate. Another advantage to riding next to him in silence was that she didn't have to worry about slipping up and mentioning something that would lead him to figuring out how old she was. She had told him she was older than he was, but she hadn't said by how much, and he hadn't asked. She found it quite gentlemanly of him not to ask. He might be a farm boy, but he had manners.

So they rode down the highway in a silence untainted by any sense of obligation. She was not his wife. She did not cook for him or do his laundry. She did not need to worry that because he was eating so many sausages at McDonald's he was going to fall over from a heart attack and die. She was not responsible for him.

With Wilbur, eating at fast food restaurants and staying at bare-bones motels, Muriel felt she was at last experiencing life stripped of its complications.

She couldn't figure out why she didn't feel bored. Perhaps it was because they were playing bridge every day in a different club, every day meeting new people, socializing with them without having the burden of real relationships. Muriel had always dreamed of doing the bridge circuit, and it was turning out to be even better than she had imagined.

They arrived at the club in Las Cruces, an adobe-colored building with a parking lot behind. They walked into the club and a man immediately walked up to her and said "Muriel? Muriel Margolin? Is it you?"

Who was this man?

"Muriel, what can it be, thirty years? More than thirty years! It's Ken Radburn!"

The name sounded vaguely familiar. Yes, it was the name of a bridge player she used to know, though not all that well.

"The last time I saw you was in Pasadena, I think. At the tournament. I even remember who your partner was. That chap from South Africa. What ever happened to him?"

"He's dead," Muriel said. She felt a celestial needle, sewing her life together. And she felt the prick of that needle.

Chapter Thirteen

Flora reached up and turned out the light.

"I can't sleep," she said, her lips brushing Jonah's naked back in the dark.

"I can," he said.

She knew he had to get up early in the morning. "Did you know that a feeling of doom is a symptom of a heart attack?" she asked him.

"Nuuuh," he half-answered, obviously trying to get her to curtail the conversation.

"Did you know that they did a study and discovered that taking statins is really effective in lowering cholesterol, and, consequently, fewer men are dying of heart attacks?"

"But next year they'll find out that they give you cancer," Jonah said, finally turning towards her.

Now she had his attention. "Worse," she said. "They found that even though a percentage of men in their study who would have died of heart disease within a given period did not do so when they took statins, the percentage of men who died within the given period remained constant."

"How can that be?" he asked, turning on his light and getting out of bed.

"They die of other things," she told him as he walked to the bathroom. "They die of safes falling out of windows and crushing their heads. They die in car crashes and in drowning accidents. They get themselves shot and they shoot themselves."

"I can't hear you," he called from the bathroom.

"It's because they have expiration dates, and there's nothing one can do about one's expiration date," she said as he crawled back into bed and tucked the sheet under his chin. "I've been thinking a lot about mine," she confessed.

"You don't have an expiration date," he said.

"How do you know?" she said.

"Well, you don't *know* your expiration date," he insisted.

"Maybe I do, and maybe I don't. But just for speculation's sake, what if I do? Isn't there anything I can do about it? What about *teshuvah, tefilah,* and *tzedakah*? Aren't they supposed to offer a way out?"

What she was referring to was the line that was repeated over and over in the High Holiday liturgy. It said that although on Rosh Hashanah, the Jewish New Year, your name was inscribed for the coming year in either the book of life or the book of death—and that on Yom Kippur your fate was sealed—if you did acts of charity, if you prayed, and if you turned back from the path that was leading you astray, then you could somehow transform the nature of the decree which proclaimed your fate. You couldn't exactly get it annulled, but you could change what it meant.

"Perhaps I should do more *teshuvah, tefilah,* and *tzedakah,*" Flora said.

"Couldn't hurt," Jonah said. "There's a story in the Talmud about a guy who avoids the Angel of Death that way."

"Who?" Flora asked. "What did he do?"

"Rabbi Eleazar. He was eating *terumah*—the special food set aside for offerings which only the priests could eat, a very great mitzvah—when the Angel showed himself to him. 'You can't take me while I'm doing such a great mitzvah,' he protested, and the Angel went away."

"I wouldn't know where to get *terumah*," Flora said.

"It doesn't exist anymore," Jonah said, "because there aren't any sacrifices anymore."

"I could try the Internet," Flora said.

"Don't bother," Jonah said, stroking Flora's head. "It's not fool-proof. There's another story in the Talmud about a guy named Rabbi Hisda. He was always studying Torah, which is such a strong mitzvah that the Angel couldn't even get near him. He studied out loud, and he never stopped reciting, so the Angel settled in a cedar tree outside the house of study. The tree cracked, Rabbi Hisda was distracted and stopped studying out loud for a moment, and the Angel overcame him."

"That story is just like the cholesterol study. So I guess there's no point in trying to do more good deeds than I normally do."

"You do plenty of good deeds," Jonah said. He put his arm around her and hugged her close. "I'm afraid there's another story in the Talmud that shows that good deeds can get you killed."

"Tell me," she said into his chest.

Jonah sighed. "Okay, there was this guy named Rabbi Hiya. Like all good rabbis, he worked really hard and was really busy. He was so busy, the Angel couldn't get an appointment with him. So one day the Angel dressed up like a poor beggar in rags and rapped on Rabbi Hiya's gate. 'Please, can I have some bread?' the Angel called out in a weak voice, and Rabbi Hiya opened the door. He couldn't resist."

"Then what happened?"

"The Angel drew his fiery sword and made Hiya yield his soul."

"Is there no hope, then?" Flora asked.

"Dear, there's always hope," Jonah said. "These are only stories. There's hope right up to the end. But in the end, everyone dies. But now I have to go to sleep," he said, and he reached up and turned out the light.

Chapter Fourteen

And so Muriel and Wilbur traveled on, from tiny town to tiny town on the bridge circuit, staying at Motel 6s and sometimes at air force bases where they could stay in the officers' quarters for practically nothing. Here they had whole suites and little kitchens, and there were laundry facilities available. The rooms were clean, if a little shabby. Then one day Wilbur suggested they take a little detour from the bridge circuit to do some sightseeing, and he turned the car toward Sedona, Arizona. Muriel agreed to this side trip on the condition that Wilbur allow her to pay for them to have some adventures—there was a train ride she had heard about near there that she had always wanted to go on, and there was also a little jaunt in an airplane they could take up to the Grand Canyon. He had been paying for everything, she told him, and she wanted it to be her treat, so he said yes.

They drove together silently across the desert. Muriel couldn't get over being able to see such a distance and with such clarity. There was a huge dark shape like a whale looming on the horizon. It was extremely far away, and yet it was utterly distinct.

She looked at the desert as they drove past, amazed by the plants. There were endless miles of what she thought must be sagebrush, all the bushes evenly spaced on the desert floor, as if planted there by some master landscaper. These gave way to miles and miles of Joshua trees, and she marveled to herself how they, also, seemed to be evenly spaced, as if they had been planted that way. She thought of the painting of the Joshua tree, Jack's favorite, leaning against the wall, waiting to be hung in her condo in Walnut Creek, in what seemed like another universe.

It was snowing when they passed the turnoff for Flagstaff. How brave Wilbur was to drive them through the snow! Finally they reached the turnoff for Sedona. It was a narrow mountain road that led them to a secret mountain valley with a river at the bottom and sheer sides rising up. There were log cabins nestled in the pine trees which looked so cozy Muriel thought she would burst with happiness. Then they came out of the snow, out of the valley, and into Sedona.

Suddenly they were in America, where everything was standardized into essential recognizable shapes. The streets were teeming with people, each life essential to itself, and here she was, Muriel Margolin, in the midst of it all. They started looking for the Motel 6. All around were beautiful red cliffs. The clouds overhead cast enormous shadows over the earth.

MURIEL AND Wilbur sat across the table from each other holding hands. They were aboard the Verde Canyon Railroad, which Muriel had always wanted to ride. How could she be feeling like she was in love with Wilbur when she was so old? She had always believed that love was reserved exclusively for the young. This was a surprise, that love was only for the young was a pack of lies, and she had bought into it. But she had never heard any old people protest that love was every bit as essential to the old as it was to the young—and every bit as possible. Old people had had their secrets which now that she had joined them she was at last privy to. It was like joining a secret society.

The other myth about seniors was that they were supposed to be repositories of wisdom, but in Muriel's estimation, they had no more wisdom than any other age group. She was just as wise now as she had ever been, which was fairly wise. People were themselves their whole lives. They didn't become something else just because they had entered old age.

As the train started to leave the station, they were served their complimentary mimosas and told they could go stand on one of the outside cars to get a better view—but they should be careful to keep their hands inside, since the canyon the train was about to traverse was quite narrow in places. After drinking her mimosa,

Muriel wanted to try the outside car. She wanted to have the full experience. Wilbur was game.

It was cold outside, and he put his arms around her to keep her warm. He didn't speak much, but he hugged. There wasn't any kissing, but the hugging felt wonderful, and Muriel was content. The red rock walls of the canyon were very close, and they were very careful to keep their hands inside the car. Then they were in a tunnel, and it smelled like damp rock; it was utterly and completely dark inside. Muriel couldn't see a thing, only feel Wilbur's arms around her. Her arms were around his belly and his arms were around her shoulders. Her face was against his. The tunnel seemed to go on forever, so that Muriel was almost afraid. Then they came out the other side.

THEY WENT back into the closed car and sat back down at their little table. The car was filled with people sitting at little tables on one side of the train and on couches around bigger tables on the other. Who were these people? What was it like to be them, to have their memories and their assumptions and their level of reality? They were all their own universes, all unknown to her; indeed, she barely knew Wilbur. At the end of the line, they made a ten-minute stop at what looked like a ghost town on a movie set. They were told it actually had been the set of a few Westerns. They went out and stood on the outside car again where some people were smoking. The engine of the train was being taken off and led onto a side track to the back of the train, which would now be the front. As the engine passed by, Muriel read the motto painted on its side: IT'S NOT THE DESTINATION, IT'S THE JOURNEY.

That was a good motto to live by. She and Wilbur didn't have any destination—they were just driving from town to town to town, avoiding the final destination, because it was harder for the Angel of Death to strike down a moving target, a target moving randomly, in places the Angel would never expect to find them. Traveling with Wilbur through the desert, Muriel was outside of danger.

It was such an old engine. That was what made it so heart-breakingly beautiful to Muriel. It was a relic from the past, but it was still running.

Everyone was taking pictures. She, herself, had bought a disposable camera on a whim, but she felt stupid pulling it out amongst all these people with their fancy digital ones. Anyway, she knew something all these younger people taking pictures didn't seem to realize—taking a picture didn't actually allow you to freeze the moment. It would never stay frozen.

They were in the home stretch of this trip, the last hours. On the train, the only person who had known her at all was Wilbur, and he barely knew her. What he knew of her was only her essence, nothing of her past or future. The sun was now low in the sky and casting shadows into the canyon.

Chapter Fifteen

Flora was outside her family's old house in Beverly Hills. There was a dog there that needed to be fed. She led him through the house to the sliding glass door that led out to the pool. The people who lived here now had made a few changes—they had installed carpet over the terrazzo in the dining room and they had reduced the pool to a small spa. Oddly enough, however, Flora found the orange melamine bowls—relics from the sixties her parents had always used to feed their cat—on the yellow counter in the kitchen, as if her mother had just finished washing them with the long-handled scrub brush she always used; as if Muriel had just removed her rubber gloves and had gone off to her study to go over some bills. But her mother had sold this house, she did not live here anymore. Flora took the bowls out to the deck and fed the dog there. The man of the house, the man who lived in the house now, graciously offered to show her around, and she took him up on the offer so she could see her old room.

Everything had been slightly modernized. The house looked nice. When she got to her old room she found it occupied by a little girl sitting on the bed. The little girl wanted Flora to quiz her for a spelling test. This Flora was happy to do. She had been a terrible speller when a child herself, something her father always criticized her for. But after years of teaching, catching other people's spelling errors, her spelling had improved, and now it was pretty good. She had taught herself tricks to remember how to spell certain words, and now she tried to teach this little girl one of these tricks. The girl had misspelled the word "scared." She had spelled it with an "i"—"scaired." "You can remember there is no 'I' in 'scared' if you say to yourself, "*I'm* not scared!" Flora told her.

That was when Flora woke up. Was she scared? What was she scared of?

FLORA HAD not heard from her mother for several days and wondered what she was up to. She wondered if she was sleeping in the same bed with her boyfriend, and she wondered if they were having sex. She didn't think she could ask her mother directly, although she wanted to know. Could people have sex in their eighties? What was there to stop it? Was there any reason not to? Certainly the idea of having to give up sex at some point was depressing. But her assumption had always been what was generally thought—that old people didn't have sex, that sex was for the young, and that even at their age she and Jonah might be unusual in continuing to have an active sex life. But perhaps people never had to give it up—at any age—but most people did because they assumed that was what they had to do, that was what was appropriate, and it was somehow unseemly to have sex after you had reached a certain age. Or perhaps most people lost their desire for sex because they believed that desire died, and believing that desire died at a certain age killed it.

This morning Flora had an appointment for her annual eye exam. She had recently gotten a mailing from the office advertising that they now did Botox treatments. It amused her that her serious-seeming doctors should be doing something so frivolous. Frivolous wasn't exactly the word she was thinking of, it was something much more insidious. When someone got Botox they could fool people into thinking that they were younger than they actually were. People would start regarding them as something they were not. Would this actually enable them to become that other thing, that younger but phony version of themselves? Botox was a toxin—maybe that was its appeal. It was a forbidden substance. It paralyzed part of your face. Flora thought, maybe it was like heroin; once you started, you couldn't stop, and it was very expensive. After a while you would start stealing from everyone you knew, or you would just accrue even more debt—that would be the civilized way to handle it.

A few years ago, these doctors had started doing LASIK surgery. One of them had had it done for himself. He looked different without glasses. She almost didn't recognize him. She had been coming to him for years, but she only saw him with her lenses off and her eyes dilated for the examination, so she didn't really know what he looked like. Once she had seen him at a party, and he had said hello, and she had said to herself, "Who's that guy?" Apparently, he hadn't wanted to wear glasses anymore even though he spent his life prescribing glasses to other people.

Flora had been wearing them since she was three years old and couldn't imagine what it would be like to suddenly have perfect vision. But she was afraid to have the surgery—afraid that she would see haloes afterward, or damage her eyes and make them even worse than they were. But perhaps she was also afraid of giving up the way she had of seeing. Without her contact lenses, everything was fuzzy to her, except things which were very close—and these were razor sharp. Would she even still be herself if she woke up from an eye operation seeing everything differently?

The woman behind the desk took her name and located her chart. "Right this way, Mrs. Rose," she said.

Flora didn't recognize her, but she only came to the office once a year. The woman had blond hair styled in an old-fashioned bouffant hairdo. She was wearing a straight skirt which came to just below her knees, dark hose, and pumps with little heels. Her persimmon lipstick was smudged. She seated Flora in front of a little machine and sat down on the other side. Apparently, she was both technician and receptionist. Flora rested her chin on the chin rest and peered into the machine eagerly. She loved this machine. When she looked into the eyepieces, she saw a farm on the horizon, at the top of a hill with a lane leading up to it. The farm was out of focus. There was a clicking, and then there it was, in perfect focus, a perfect farmhouse. Looking at it filled her with an odd delight. She wondered if her mother was feeling this strange delight on her road trip with her farm-boy, Wilbur.

The technician then led Flora to an examination room to wait for the doctor. It began to dawn on Flora that the technician was a transsexual. Her voice was low, and her wrists and feet were very large. As she was leaving the room, she bumped the mirror on the wall and then turned back into the room to right it. She had absolutely no hips or behind.

In a few minutes, the doctor came in and had her rest her chin in the chin rest and look into the instrument. She could see where letters were projected into the mirror that hung from the wall in front of her. "Is this better or is this better?" he kept asking her, changing the lenses. They made a distinctive snapping sound as they slipped back and forth. Flora looked at the letters in the mirror, trying to decide which lens was clearer. What did the letters spell? She couldn't decipher them. They spelled out words, it seemed, which could only be understood in another realm, the world on the other side of the mirror.

A mirror was a portal to the underworld, where everything was the same, only backwards and upside down. Flora was the only nearsighted person in her whole extended family—except for her Aunt Sonja. Her mother had often compared her to her aunt for this reason. Aunt Sonja had been the homeliest and least successful of all their relatives. All her life Flora had felt she had somehow failed her mother by being nearsighted. Now her mother was on a road trip—she was the Jack Kerouac of mothers—she was on a road trip with her boyfriend and she wasn't thinking of Flora. She hadn't called in several days. When she did call and Flora complained that she hadn't called, she said, "Oh, I didn't want to bother you. You're so busy." But Flora didn't buy this. She thought her mother just wasn't interested in her, that she didn't feel about her the way Flora felt about her own children. On the other hand, maybe she had decided to give Flora her freedom—freedom from the daily worry about a loved one.

Both of Flora's girls had been over for dinner the night before. After dinner, they went upstairs to get ready to go out to a party. Flora had come in to watch them put on makeup and preen in front of the mirror. She had stood transfixed, looking at them;

they were both so beautiful and so sultry. They were laughing at each other's mirror-faces. They loved to laugh at Flora and Jonah's mirror-faces, the faces they assumed only when they looked at themselves in a mirror, the masks which protected them from the world on the other side of the mirror. They did not want to go behind the mirror yet. Flora did not want to go. She wanted to see her children marry, she wanted to be a grandmother. But it was already May, and she had only four months left. How could she leave her daughters? They had lied in the cosmic courtroom. At twenty-four and twenty-three, her daughters weren't ready to live in the world without her. She would lift a Volkswagen off of them if one were on top of them. Their lives were more important than hers to her.

Chapter Sixteen

Muriel awoke alone in her bed at the Motel 6 in Sedona with a pain in her groin. Wilbur was already dressed, sitting on the other bed, working on his bridge system. He was a farmer, and always woke up before dawn, despite the fact that there were no cows for him to milk here in Sedona. Indeed, she had no idea whether there had even been cows on the farm he had grown up on. She had only heard about the mules, and certainly they didn't need to be milked. Maybe he just had trouble sleeping. Maybe his sleep had been disturbed by his wife dying on him. Muriel had no way of knowing. He didn't talk.

Yesterday, at her instigation and insistence that it be her treat, they had gone on a jeep tour of the surrounding area. The ride had been extremely bumpy, and each time they were jolted into the air her seat belt had dug into her groin. That was the explanation for the pain she was feeling there this morning, she was sure. The jeep trip was interesting. They had learned that there were seventeen varieties of rattlesnake in the area, but that because it was winter, they were all sleeping. It's lucky that we're here in the winter, Muriel had thought.

When Wilbur told her that he had been a pilot while they were sitting together on that big round hassock in the hotel lobby in Colorado, the desire to have him fly her in a plane had overwhelmed her. Since he had to retire from flying, however, when she saw the advertisement for a trip in a small plane from Sedona to the Grand Canyon, she had signed them up.

Muriel climbed out of bed and went to the window to peek out the curtain. The sky looked dark and menacing. Perhaps today was not a good day to go up in a small plane. She worried that Wilbur was just being polite by agreeing to go up in the plane with her today. She worried that he wasn't really interested in flying with her. She suspected he was eager to get back to the bridge circuit. How could she know what he wanted when he never spoke?

They had a cup of coffee and an Egg McMuffin at McDonald's before driving to the little airport. Muriel was getting used to eating at fast food places. The food was cheap and plentiful, and the ambiance unpretentious, if somewhat hideous. And having changed her habits like this, she almost felt like she had slipped into another life—evading her own, which was on a trajectory going rapidly in one direction, to a destination she was trying to avoid.

After they had breakfasted, they drove to the airport, which was at the very end of Airport Drive, of course. The weather now looked even more threatening to Muriel, but she assumed they wouldn't fly if it wasn't safe, no matter how eager for her tourist dollars they happened to be. Their pilot hadn't arrived yet, the man behind the counter told them. He was stuck in traffic. Meanwhile, he would take care of all the paperwork. He wanted to know how much they each weighed.

Muriel told him, lying by a mere five pounds. But then she couldn't believe how much Wilbur weighed, when he said it out loud. He did have a pot belly zipped inside his jumpsuit. What was she doing with a man with a potbelly? She had always despised people who carried extra weight. What was happening to her?

Finally, the pilot arrived, a wiry little man with silver hair. He led them out to a little red biplane on the runway. They would be taking this little four-seater instead of one of the larger planes because Muriel and Wilbur were their only customers this morning. Everyone else had cancelled.

It was the cutest airplane Muriel had ever seen. The pilot helped them into their seats, and then he helped them adjust the earphones they had to wear. The earphones helped buffer the loud sound of the engine and enabled them to communicate with each other, as each had a microphone. Had the other people cancelled because they knew something, like that it was too dangerous to fly today? Muriel asked, speaking into the microphone. As usual, Wilbur was silent. "I wouldn't fly today if I thought it was too dangerous," the pilot told them. "I don't want to die."

The plane lifted from the ground, seemingly without effort, and suddenly they were floating over the world, over the red rock formations reaching into the sky. Coming toward them was a big, black cloud.

They were about to fly into a cloud of snow when the pilot decided they better go back. Muriel didn't mind. The trip, though brief, had been terrific. They had floated over the world, very low, over the projections of red rock, each with its distinctive shape. She felt high. The trip lasted about forty-five minutes, and then they were back on the ground. They would reschedule and take the whole trip tomorrow, when the weather was going to be better. This was just a bonus.

When they were back in the airport, they made their arrangements and walked out to the parking lot. Little flakes of snow were falling down.

As soon as they were back in the room Wilbur returned to working on his bridge system. "Why don't we take a walk?" Muriel said. She was getting bored. "They said there's a trail to one of the vortexes right outside our door."

"What is a vortex?"

"Well, I guess we'll find out when we get there."

They set out on the trail. It was a narrow path over red dirt, climbing a hill between cactuses and other spiny things. Soon they could see spread out beneath them the back parking lot of the huge Walgreen's at the end of the street their motel was on. But spread out around and above them were the craggy red rock cliffs that Muriel had seen in countless commercials and Westerns. After about a half hour of silent walking, the trail ended at a road. They climbed the barricade and crossed it. Across the road was a sign indicating they had come to a vortex, a place that was supposed to have special energy. Muriel had seen the Airport Loop Trail on a map, and assumed this was the trailhead.

The snow had stopped, so they set out. The first hundred yards involved climbing over smooth slippery rock sloping steeply upward. At the top was a narrow ledge to walk along, overlooking a steep drop—a mountainside peppered with spiny cactus.

Muriel was afraid to look down. Her knees were weak. "I don't think I can do this," she said. "I think I'll have to go back."

"Okay, we'll go back," Wilbur said, and he took her hand.

They crossed the road again, and then climbed back over the barricade and continued back down the hill. After they had been walking for a few minutes, they came to another trail marker for the Airport Loop Trail. They had somehow overlooked this on the way up.

"This must be the beginning of the loop. We must have been at the end," Wilbur said.

"This looks like a lot nicer trail. There's not such a scary drop-off," she said.

"It looks very easy," he said.

"Of course it could get scarier further down the trail," she said.

"I don't think so. It looks pretty wide," he said.

"But it's going to get scary at the end. We just saw the end."

"But I bet that part is only a few feet, and then you're past it, on this nice wide trail. Do you want to try it?" he asked.

"Okay, we can always turn back if it gets too scary," she said.

"It's not going to get too scary," he said, walking ahead of her.

She felt like she had been finessed. The trail was not all that wide. There was room only for one person at a time. But she liked watching him from behind. He was so unlike anyone she had ever been with before. He had put on an old canvas jacket over his jumpsuit. Because she had to spend most of her time looking down at the trail, looking where she put her feet, she could only afford to snatch brief glances at him. Everything on the trail was spindly and spiky. She watched as Wilbur's pants legs brushed against the cactuses. He wasn't watching where he was going. He was inside his head, up in the clouds. She was glad it was winter. All the snakes were sleeping in their lairs. "Wake up, snakes," she said softly, to herself. She wouldn't mind seeing just one.

"I have to pee," she said aloud.

"So do I," he answered, stepping off the trail and down behind a tree.

Muriel found a little space without cactuses behind another tree, dropped her pants, and positioned herself facing uphill so she would not get pee on her shoes. It felt incredible to pee outside. It made her feel like she was part of nature, like she was an animal.

Now she felt a lot better, even ready to encounter some wild animal, like the wild pig she had heard about that roamed here. She marched merrily along the trail. The hill started to descend more and more, but it didn't scare her, possibly because the descent had been gradual, she'd had time to get used to it. She knew that really there was no going back, they had gone too far, and when they arrived at the narrow ledge she would have to cross it, so she would. The important thing was not to be afraid.

When they arrived there she knew there was a possibility that she would miss her footing and tumble into the abyss. She wondered if that was what they meant by vortex, something that pulled you into it like a black hole. Nothing that went into a black hole ever came out again.

But she didn't fall into it. It wasn't her time yet. She still had some unfinished business here on earth, apparently. She still had some unfulfilled desires.

BACK AT the motel, Muriel noticed that there were some cactus spines poking out of Wilbur's pant leg. She bent down and started to pull them out. Then he unzipped his jumpsuit and stepped out of it. There were several cactus spines sticking right out of his leg. Carefully and purposefully, she began to pull them out, kneeling in front of him.

Chapter Seventeen

Flora was thinking about all the possible ways she might die. It was already June. She had only a few months left now, according to the dream, which wasn't a dream, but was real. It didn't appear that she was going to die of any disease that took more than a few months to run its course because she didn't have more than a few months. She was pretty sure most diseases took more than that to get to the endgame. That was one of the worst things about them—that you had to suffer before dying. Dying was bad enough all by itself. And to spend your last few months on earth going through rounds of treatments rather than doing the things you had always wanted to do, and had never been able to—it wasn't fair. And yet, perhaps there was something about being in pain and having to spend your last minutes in the middle of a medical procedure that was just as good—or maybe even better than being able to live out your dreams, to slowly and effortlessly slip away into the dust. You might not be so reluctant to die, then. There was always the chance. The truth was usually surprising.

Would the proximate cause of Flora's demise be cancer? That was unlikely. Cancer usually took more than a few months to kill you. Heart disease? People were always keeling over from heart disease they never knew they had, dropping dead on the tennis court. But Flora did not play tennis.

Luckily, it was almost impossible for Flora to die of Alzheimer's, the way her mother-in-law had. She still had most of her marbles, and Alzheimer's was painfully slow. That was something to be thankful for.

There were influenzas, of course, that came on suddenly and killed people within a few days, burning them up with enormously high fevers so that their inner organs literally turned to soup. Then there were the flesh-eating diseases, where you could watch your flesh being devoured before your eyes until you were no more. And these things happened to people. Flora knew someone whose boyfriend had had the flesh-eating disease. He didn't die, but it broke up their relationship. She just couldn't get over her aversion to his fleshless extremities.

There were sudden brain tumors, and the doctors saying, *there's nothing we can do, it's too dangerous to operate. We would have to slice through the brain to get to the tumor.* And slicing through the brain is like putting a hacksaw through a circuit board. You might survive the operation, the cancer might be eradicated and you'd be cancer-free, but your whole brain would be disconnected. You'd be a vegetable.

There was also liver failure, of course. One couldn't go very long without a functioning liver. But what made the liver fail was a mystery. Flora didn't know anyone who had died of liver disease.

There were undoubtedly many other fast-acting diseases Flora didn't know about that could kill her by her expiration date, but she couldn't think of any. She kind of thought the proximate cause of her death would have to be an accident, a dire one. They happened all the time. Bricks fell off of buildings and smashed in people's heads. People fell into machines at meat-packing plants. They drove off road and exploded in a fiery ball, drunk drivers careened into them in the middle of the desert, chunks of metal fell from bridges they were driving under, killing them—but not their spouse who was driving and didn't suffer a scratch. People walked into caves for fun, exploring them, and got lost and couldn't find their way out, and they starved to death.

There were countless ways Flora might die by accident. Most of the time you could avoid them, just not that last one, lying in wait for you.

"I don't think I'm going to die of a disease," Flora said. She was sitting on the plush loveseat in their bedroom trying to unwind before going to sleep. She needed a half hour or so of conversation with Jonah before going to bed. Jonah was lying on the bed watching a basketball game.

"Are you still holding on to that dream? I can't wait till you turn sixty. Then you'll see that the dream wasn't really true, that you were not really given an expiration date," he said.

"It *was* true," she said.

"What makes you so sure?"

"Well, it was because of who was in the dream. They were behind this little wooden balustrade that was the separation between *here* and *there*, the world and the underworld, this world and the next. They were all in the next world, where they were going to be in twenty-five years, by the time of my expiration date. They were testifying from beyond the grave, from a place where they had perfect vision."

Flora paused and then said, "Your grandmother didn't last very long, did she? That was a sad death, a very sad death. Everybody loved her so. And then there was your father's death. I know that was really hard on you. I think that's why you got sick after he died. Your immune system was compromised. What's it been? Twenty years? But I think my father's death was quite satisfying, in its way. I had all those years after they moved here to make my peace with him, to tell him I loved him. I didn't feel there was anything undone when he died. He did not protest death, he went along with it nobly. And we were all there. As deaths go, I think it was excellent. But your mother's death was rather horrifying, even though we had even more time to prepare for it. I guess Alzheimer's is the worst. I think her heart just forgot how to beat."

"I wonder what your mother's death will be like," Jonah said.

Flora leapt to her feet. "Oh, my God!" she said. "I can't believe it. I just realized something! My mother is still alive!"

"You just realized that?"

"No! What I mean is, she's not supposed to be alive! According to the dream, she was supposed to be behind that little wooden balustrade by now. She's supposed to be dead like all the others! And you know, God's been sending his hit man after her—what about that rogue wave, what about being dragged by a car—something's been after her! But she's evading it—better than those rabbis in the Talmud! And you know what?"

"What?"

"The dream can't be true as long as my mother's alive! Because she can't be on the other side of the balustrade until she's dead! So, as long as she's alive, the dream isn't true and my expiration date isn't my sixtieth birthday!"

"I never believed it was. But I'm relieved to know it isn't."

"You know something? I always thought my mother wasn't too interested in my welfare, but now I see she's actually a super-mother. She's doing more than lifting a Volkswagen off of me; she's fending off the Angel of Death for me. She's standing between me and *It*.

"You think she's staying alive for your sake?"

"Well, probably not consciously. But that doesn't matter. She's doing a really good job of it. I think I love her more than I have in my whole life."

"Where is your mother?"

"I'm not exactly sure. Somewhere in Arizona, I think. She hasn't called in a while. She's on a road trip with a strange man. I think she's having the time of her life."

Chapter Eighteen

This time their pilot was waiting for them inside the airport. He was chatting it up with a glamorous if hard-looking Russian woman. She was wearing tight jeans and high-heeled boots, and the pilot was standing over her, toeing the rug with one sneakered foot. The Russian woman, who looked to be somewhere in her thirties, had blond hair framing her white, white face and red, red lips. Her bored middle-school-aged daughter, who wore jeans and a pink sweatshirt, lounged nearby. Standing menacingly at the counter was the great grey hulk of a man, her father, who was visiting from the Ukraine and didn't speak a word of English. Muriel had heard the blond tell the pilot this in her thick Russian accent. She lived in Washington, D.C., and he had spent a week with her there, and now they were all on a road trip. Apparently, this little family was going on their own jaunt to the Grand Canyon. Yesterday, she and Wilbur had been the only people on the trip. Now they would be sharing the experience with these people.

"We're just waiting for a couple more folks," the man who was to be their pilot today told them. Muriel's family had come from the Ukraine originally, in the 1880s. They had immigrated here to get away from the Ukrainians who liked to get drunk, rape, and disembowel Jews. But this giant had no way of knowing she was Jewish. Then the couple they must have been waiting for walked into the room. Somewhere in their sixties, they were also behemoths.

Muriel didn't know why she found huge people so frightening. Perhaps it was because she knew they could crush her, if they chose to. Wilbur was large, and his size put a little zest into their relationship, a slight element of fear that kept it interesting. But these people made him look small. They could eat him for dinner.

It turned out the last couple to arrive were from Alberta. They both wore blue jeans. He was wearing a cowboy hat and an immense black jacket with leather sleeves and the insignia of his labor union on the back. She had bright red nails, large ones, on the ends of fingers laden with ornate rings. Perhaps she thought that bringing attention to her hands would keep people from noticing how large she was, Muriel opined. If Muriel were as massive as this woman she would kill herself, but that thought had probably never crossed this woman's mind. She was large and homely, and a perfect match for her bulky husband. Apparently, where she came from, one simply accepted one's homeliness without any expectation that things could have been different.

Muriel found such fatalism depressing. The gaudy rings on the woman's fingers made Muriel suspect that they had struck it rich in oil; that was what Alberta was known for, she seemed to remember. So now they were rich and traveling to the Grand Canyon for a holiday, because that's what people did when they had made all their money and their grandchildren were getting old and they still had a little life in them. They were going to see something extraordinary so that when the time came to die they wouldn't have to say, "I'm dying, and I never saw the Grand Canyon." They thought if they saw the Grand Canyon now, before they were on their deathbeds, they would be able to die in peace when they came to the end of the line.

The pilot, who was not the grizzled, wiry pilot Muriel and Wilbur had had yesterday, was a man of about forty with a military haircut. He led them out to a small silver plane. Muriel was sorry they weren't going in the biplane again, but it was too small to take them all, these eight people who had been brought together for some purpose by fate. The pilot started arranging them by weight, to balance the load. Muriel was placed behind the incredible Ukrainian hulk. She was going to have to look at his craggy, cold, murderous profile all the way to the Grand Canyon. Wilbur was seated behind her, silent as usual. Through the window, out of the corner of her eye, she saw the pilot climbing up the wing. Was this how a pilot normally climbed into the cockpit, she wondered?

Finally, when everyone put on their seatbelts, the plane droned into the air. Then Muriel heard the pilot talking to them through the earphones. He told them what was beneath them—all the evocative names of the red rock formations—and he told them about himself. He had just returned from Iraq and Afghanistan. He had spent a lot of time in these hot spots. He was not at liberty to tell them what he had been doing there—just that the pay was very, very good. This information gave Muriel some confidence that the pilot knew what he was doing and the plane wouldn't crash, but also made her wonder how inclined to take chances this guy might be.

After another half-hour they landed safely on the south rim of the Grand Canyon. Handlers were there to help them out and to hustle them into the gift shop, which was filled with tourists from Las Vegas, who were mostly Japanese. They would go home satisfied that they had seen the real America. Muriel picked up a little papoose doll and turned it over. It was made in China. After they had time to shop, their little group was led out onto the tarmac, arrayed in a line, and instructions about helicopter safety were read out loud to them. They were each given a card with these instructions in several languages. The most important instruction was not to get too close to the back of the helicopter, because if you did, the rotors might slice you to ribbons. They were then hustled to where the helicopters were waiting and helped inside.

Muriel got the shotgun seat. The pilot seemed to be a mere boy, a boy playing with military toys. That was why people volunteered to fight in Iraq, Muriel thought. It was because of the toys, these wonderful toys. The helicopter was all transparent plastic. It was quite beautiful and riding in it was like floating on air. It lifted up, and then it floated down into the canyon, staying close to one wall, so close that Muriel could have reached out and touched a cactus clinging to it. It was amazing, like being an insect.

But all too soon, they were at the bottom of the canyon where handlers were helping them out and away from the slashing propellers, down a wooden staircase to the Colorado River where more handlers were waiting to help them onto boats. Their boat took off, and they were going down the river with other boats ahead, behind and to each side, with helicopters rising and falling all around them. After about twenty minutes the boat stopped, and the boat pilot asked them if they wanted their pictures taken. He took a picture of each party with their own cameras, so when they got home, they could put a picture in their album showing them floating in a peaceful boat down the Colorado River at the bottom of the Grand Canyon. In the picture, there was no deafening helicopter noise. In the picture, they would be alone in the boat in the river in the canyon forever. Anyone looking at the picture, including themselves, would imagine that they had spent endless hours in the boat by themselves in the river in the canyon.

But as soon as the last picture was snapped, the boat was turned around and they sped back to the platform at the wooden staircase where handlers were waiting to help them out. They were on the river a total of forty minutes. They climbed the wooden staircase again where, at the top, handlers were ready to help them back into a helicopter, which carried them back up to the rim of the canyon in a matter of minutes.

That was what her life had been like—it had all gone so quickly, and soon she would die, and then she would ride in a helicopter or some other heavenly conveyance up to the rim.

After they had been helped out of the helicopter and had avoided walking into the rotors, they were led to a bus which was waiting to take them to where the Indians were going to serve them lunch, up at Guano Point. Their pilot was with them on the bus. He told them they should present their lunch tickets when they arrived, and he described what they would be eating: corn on the cob, coleslaw, meat, beans, cornbread, and, his personal favorite, peach cobbler. After lunch they could take a short walk out on Guano Point. He personally recommended it.

Muriel made her way through the lunch line. She loved cornbread, and she loved peach cobbler. The meat looked weird, and she didn't take any. The Indians who served her were all obese and sickly looking. They were all so downtrodden it was difficult

117

for Muriel to look at them. Yet they made their living by getting tourists to look at them.

She followed Wilbur out to a picnic table. Wilbur's plate was piled high. He did not seem to find the meat questionable. The pilot came and sat down at their table.

"So, you mind if I join you?" he asked.

"Aren't you going to eat?" Muriel asked.

"No, I'm trying to lose about thirty pounds."

"Thirty pounds!" Muriel said. "You can't mean that. You're in great shape."

"No, I've put on thirty pounds since I got back from Afghanistan."

"How was it there?"

"Oh, it was crazy. I liked Germany a lot better."

Muriel didn't say anything. When she thought of Germany, she thought of gas chambers.

"So, you want to take that little walk out to Guano Point?"

"Okay," Wilbur said.

Muriel went to dump their paper plates in the big trash can. The Russian woman seemed to be having a fight with her daughter, who was sitting on the rim of the canyon, dangling her feet over the side. There was no guardrail, only a precipitous drop into a beckoning void. Just seeing her sitting there gave Muriel the chills. How could her mother let her put herself in so much danger? Perhaps she thought that because this was a tourist attraction, it had to be safe, despite appearances. Perhaps she thought it wasn't real, that it was just an illusion, a sort of Las Vegas. Perhaps she thought her daughter couldn't fall to her death, or that death itself wasn't real.

Wilbur and the pilot were already walking down the trail, and she hurried to catch up with them. The trail led them down and onto a narrow peninsula that led out into the canyon. Muriel was all right as long as she just looked at the feet of the pilot ahead of her and didn't look up or to either side. Because if she looked up she would have to see that ahead of them the peninsula simply ended in midair, thousands of feet above the floor of the canyon;

118

and if she looked to either side she would see that if she made any missteps in either direction she would fall into the maw, the void that wanted her to fall into it, which was always calling out to her in a voice she was careful to turn a deaf ear to.

The Russian woman was now walking behind her, and the Canadian couple followed in the rear. It made Muriel feel uneasy to have them bunching up behind her. Soon they came to a place where the peninsula got significantly narrower, and the pilot stopped. Muriel took Wilbur's hand to steady herself. The pilot waited for everybody else to come up to him and stop, then he leapt over the edge, out over the abyss, before coming to roost on a tiny rock outcropping only wide enough for him to perch on one foot. He stood poised there for a heart-stopping moment— then he jumped back to where they were standing.

"Oh, I don't have my camera!" the Russian woman lamented. "Let me go beck and get my camera—and my fadher. Could you do it again? I'll be right beck." She hurried off in her high-heeled boots.

In a few minutes she was back with her camera and her father, and the pilot made his death defying leap for her twice more. Each time he jumped, Muriel felt sick to her stomach. She wanted to run off the promontory altogether, but she was too terrified to move, and could barely manage to maneuver herself to a big rock at the center of the path and press herself up against it as hard as she could. She wondered who was watching the Russian woman's daughter and how the woman didn't seem at all concerned that her daughter might fall from the perch on the rim of the canyon where she had left her.

It was fascinating, if horrifying, to watch the pilot balancing on one foot over the abyss. Could it be that he didn't care if he fell to his death? Did he want to scare them into thinking they were going to see someone fall to his death? Or was it that he was addicted to the feeling he got when he knew that death was imminent? It could be that for him knowing that death was imminent was the ultimate high. Yes, as she looked at him balancing over the chasm she saw that it was true—he was higher than a kite.

Chapter Nineteen

They were on their way to San Quentin to protest the execution that was supposed to take place that night. Flora usually went with Jonah on these dire occasions, to stand outside the gates and protest. It had always been clear to her that capital punishment was wrong. The executions were invariably scheduled for one minute past midnight, one minute into the day the court mandated that the prisoner was to die. "Why do they have to do it in the middle of the night?" Flora asked Jonah, as they were leaving the house well bundled in warm clothes.

"The state must be really eager to kill someone," Jonah answered.

"I think they schedule them when they do because midnight's such a ghoulish hour," Flora said.

"Maybe they do it at midnight so most people will be asleep when they're taking place," Jonah suggested. "So they can do it without people even being aware of it."

That was why he always made a speech at the protest rally, so the press would cover it and awareness would be raised.

Jonah made a speech in protest no matter who was being executed. It didn't matter to him how murderous or how possibly innocent the convict was. This horrific event wasn't really about the person being executed. He might be a heinous murderer, but to Jonah, that was beside the point. Executing a perpetrator of a violent crime was itself a violent act. Executions only served to create more violence in the world.

What bothered Flora was that the execution was being carried out by the state. The state was every person in it. If the state put a person to death, every person in the state was perforce a murderer, and Flora didn't want to be a murderer. When Jonah made his speech, standing on the platform, he would point out this irony. People thought they had the right to kill someone who had killed others. But if murder was wrong, why did people think it wasn't wrong if *they* did it? Didn't they realize that allowing capital punishment turned all the citizens of the state into murderers? Didn't they see that the solution to the problem of violence in the world could never be the creation of more violence?

The executions had been happening with increasing frequency and were starting to become routine. Flora and Jonah knew from experience they had to dress warmly, because it was always cold in the dead of night outside the gates of San Quentin. They left the house at about 10:30 in fleece jackets, knit caps, gloves, and scarves. This was about the time they usually went to sleep. They drove across the bridge and had to park fairly far away from the prison and walk up the hill in the dark.

Shapes of other people appeared ahead of them in the fog, and soon they were walking in a crowd. People walked silently or spoke in low tones, in deference to the solemnity of the occasion, yet there was also an undercurrent of excitement in the crowd mounting the hill. More and more, these executions felt like medieval fairs, some sort of giant party honoring the imminence of death

Flora could never understand how the Supreme Court could have voted capital punishment back into law, or how it could later have been validated by the state referendum by a seventy percent majority. Clearly, people were angry and afraid. Some wanted retribution. They thought they could balance the scales of justice themselves, that it was within their power. She also wondered if, on another level, the voters were so overwhelmed by the horror of contemplating their own deaths, they felt—superstitiously—that if they could see to it that someone else died, that death would somehow substitute for their own. This was absurd, of course, because no one's death could take the place of anyone else's— everyone was bound to die and would suffer his or her own death in due course, Flora thought.

Lately, the executions had been theme-based. The last one had been of a reformed gang leader. That had been the most glamorous execution Flora had yet attended. Elegant black men in full-length caramel-colored leather coats with state-of-the-art sound equipment had choreographed the speeches. The crowd was so huge there literally was nowhere to move. Jonah and she had to squeeze their way to the platform. The press was there from all over the world.

This time the execution was all about Native Americans. When Flora and Jonah reached the top of the hill, they found tribal elders chanting and beating drums. A group of Buddhists were sitting in meditation on one side, and behind them a group of hecklers with signs calling for an eye for an eye; but the people in favor of the execution were clearly in the minority here. They didn't need to come, after all. Those who wanted bloodshed, who believed in the efficacy of retribution, had already prevailed. The crowd filled the area in front of the gate, and speeches and announcements came through the public address system that had been erected. There were some houses here by the gate—pleasant old Craftsmen-style houses with front porches, and some of the people who had come for the execution were sitting on their steps. Flora wondered who lived in these pleasant houses with a view of the bay in one direction and a view of the prison in the other. Was this where the guards and wardens lived, raising their families?

Those protesting the execution—standing in the freezing cold listening to speech after speech—would hold onto a little hope in their hearts for a last-minute reprieve from the governor, right up until one minute past midnight. The speeches were sometimes moving, personal testimony about the goodness of the prisoner. At other times they were self-serving political diatribes delivered by representatives of one group or another. Jonah's speech was usually the only one which dealt with spiritual issues.

Tonight there was a lot of chanting, and there was a nobility in the native elders' speeches. There were also speeches by lawyers pointing out the racism that singled out Native Americans and other people of color for the sacrifice. Flora was getting colder and colder waiting for Jonah's turn. He always spoke last, right at the end. It made her a little nervous listening to him because she worried that he would be speaking when the execution started, and she felt that would be disrespectful, that there should be silence at that moment. But he finished at exactly one minute past midnight, the moment when it was clear that all hope was lost, no reprieve had come.

Reprieves seldom came, however. The execution was now in progress somewhere behind the gate. A bright light was shining on the crowd, blinding Flora, and there was the deafening sound of a motor. Was it the generator for the light and the PA system, or was it a noise the prison made to drown out the songs of this solemn gathering? Was it the sound of the death machine at work inside the prison? She didn't know.

Now the waiting began. The first time Flora attended an execution she had expected a representative from the prison to come over to the gate at five minutes after twelve to tell them that the prisoner was dead—but that never happened. No such announcement was ever made. They had stood in the dark and the cold waiting for forty minutes until they heard the news on a portable radio that the prisoner was dead.

But it also took forty minutes because it had taken almost that long for the state to execute the prisoner. Why did it take so long to kill him, Flora wondered? When their dog was dying the vet had shaved a little place on his flank, where the muscles had already atrophied, and they had all petted him and told him they loved him as she gave him a lethal injection. He was dead within a few minutes, his old blind eyes glazed over. Why did it take so long to kill a human being? Why did they always botch it?

Jonah always insisted that they stay until the announcement came that the prisoner was dead. As a rabbi, he had presided over the funerals of countless people, and he always remained at the graveside long after the mourners had departed, to watch until the grave was completely filled up. He always told people that the dirt with which the coffin was covered up was like the blanket loving parents pull up over their children to tuck them in at night, telling them to sleep tight, wishing them sweet dreams.

But tonight Jonah was tired, and, to Flora's surprise, at twenty after twelve he asked Flora if she was ready to leave. She was freezing. She did want to go, but it worried her that Jonah was losing his need to show respect for the dead. She was worried that these executions were becoming just a normal part of life, of the monthly routine.

Flora also wondered if she wasn't becoming a little bit addicted to these executions, for although on one level it was aggravating to have to go out at 10:30 at night in the freezing cold, it was also exciting to be out in the middle of the night. On their walk up the hill, there was a turn in the road where Flora always realized that this road was overlooking the bay, that this spot was without doubt one of the most beautiful places in the world. And she felt the terrible irony that this road dead-ended at a horrible prison with a ghastly killing chamber.

Now as Flora and Jonah descended the road hand in hand, she saw the stars gleaming on the bay beneath them. Flora thought of her own reprieve, the stay of execution, the cancellation of her expiration date which her mother had gained for her, defying every effort of the Angel of Death to get at her, maintaining her position between her daughter and *It*. At last they reached their car, and soon they were driving back toward the Golden Gate Bridge. The fog was dense, so dense that they couldn't see they were on the bridge, even when they knew they were. Jonah took off his gloves and turned on the radio for news of the execution. The prisoner had been pronounced dead at 12:35. Jonah reached for Flora's hand. Beneath them the dark water was rushing under the bridge and out into the vast sea.

Chapter Twenty

Muriel had to face the fact that she hadn't called her daughters in several days. She had been so enjoying not being in touch with Flora or Daphne or anyone else from the world of entanglements and commitments and emotional involvement, away from the world with its long history, its regrets and anxieties, the things it felt wonderful not to feel—but not because she didn't love her daughters. Of course she loved them—they were her daughters. That wasn't what this was about. This was about floating free, letting go. Traveling with Wilbur she was freed even of the obligation to talk.

But she had to call her daughters now, so they wouldn't worry. She had to step for a moment back into her past life and all its complications, back out of this large, heavy American car with its deep sagging upholstery upon which she was perched as Wilbur drove the two of them down the empty highway. They had left Sedona several hours ago and now they were headed back to the bridge circuit. Muriel picked up her bag and pulled out her cell phone.

How she loved her cell phone. She laughed when she thought how she had resisted having one. Daphne had sent her one, but she had sent it right back to her, saying she didn't think she could ever figure out how to use it—she was too old. Daphne had sent her another one, and she had sent that one back, too, saying she didn't think she would ever have a use for it, that she was considering just getting one that called 911 like the one she had seen advertised in her AAA magazine. Then Daphne sent her another one, and finally she gave in.

She soon discovered it was actually easy to use. There was nothing to it. She used it first to call Flora from BART to let her know she was on her way, so Flora would go to the library to meet her; and then to call Daphne when she was out walking. And at last, she started using it all the time. She enjoyed being able to call anyone from anywhere, and it was a thrill that people wouldn't know where she was calling from. This meant she could be anywhere. She didn't have to be tied to that flimsy transparent cord that came out of the wall of her condo in Laurel Dell anymore.

Both Daphne and Flora's machines answered. Muriel had called them on their landlines hoping this would happen, because she didn't really want to talk to them. She just wanted to do her duty and let them know she was okay. After she left the message she closed her phone and put it back into her bag, and she put her bag back on the floor.

How she wished she could be on vacation like this forever. It wouldn't last forever, of course, because at some point Wilbur would find out how old she was, and he would dump her.

Muriel's deepest desire was not to have to worry about anybody or anything. She was relieved they were going back on the circuit again. In some ways, playing a game of bridge was the surest method of suspending life and its terrible reality, as if preserving it in amber. Muriel didn't like life to feel too real. When it was too real, it was scary. Now that she had discharged her duty and called her daughters, life felt just the right amount of real, and she wanted it never to end.

That morning while they were eating their silent breakfast at McDonald's, she had read in the paper that in another 100 years people living to the age of 200 would be commonplace. She had been thinking, lately, that at the rate she was going, she could easily live to 100. But now she saw that wasn't very long compared to what people would get to enjoy in another 100 years, and she felt jealous of them. But she wondered if the longevity prediction had factored in the effects of global warming. Possibly in 100 years there would be no earth left on which to live long. There would be no glaciers left to melt, only roving bands of cannibals darting over a landscape where nothing was growing. How many 200-year-old people could there be enjoying their longevity under those conditions? Probably not many, if any at all. Perhaps she was quite fortuitously alive at the most optimal time in history.

Yes, this really was the time to be alive—when one could live longest—before the great destruction. It was too bad for her grandchildren, but they had all lived spoiled lives. Muriel had lived through the Great Depression. She had paid her dues, so she deserved whatever pleasure she was able to experience now.

They arrived at a strange little town in the desert and pulled into the Motel 6. It was getting late, and Wilbur was tired. He did all the driving, although she could have spelled him, but he was old-fashioned that way. That was one of the things she liked about him. Tomorrow they would head back to Texas for the bridge circuit. This little sightseeing detour had been fine, but they were both eager to get back to the card table.

When they got to their room, Muriel walked to the window and pulled back the drapes. There in the parking lot below a jackrabbit sped by, through the sagebrush just in front of the car. The endless desert stretched back behind the rabbit. The power, speed, size, and wildness of this animal gave Muriel a little thrill. "Look!" she said to Wilbur, who was sitting on the bed poring over his notes for his bridge system.

"What?" he asked, looking up for a moment.

"Never mind," she said. "It's gone. You missed it."

FOR DINNER, they went to a Chinese fast food place she picked because it was part of a chain she had never been to before, though she had seen them in strip malls and airports for years. She had assumed that the food at this chain would be bland and disgusting, and she was very pleasantly surprised to find that it was actually bland and delicious. They took their trays to a plastic table for two, and while Muriel looked around at the other customers, Wilbur silently spooned fried rice and pork into his mouth. She wondered if it bothered him that the food was Chinese. He wouldn't buy anything that wasn't made in America. Maybe he didn't want to eat any food that wasn't American, either, but he hadn't protested.

The restaurant was packed with people. Across from them was seated what seemed to be a large, extended family of cute little Asian people from some unidentifiable Asian place—Vietnam, maybe. They were all giggling gaily, and their adorable tiny tots were racing around them between the tables, laughing. Next to Muriel and Wilbur was a young white family with three children under the age of four. This chain must be a good place to bring children, Muriel guessed, or else everyone in this town had small children. Muriel loved eating at a place where there were children, not just old people eating the Early Bird Special, like at the high-class restaurants she had often gone to with Pauline and Pierre back in Walnut Creek.

This family she was now staring at looked to her to be trailer trash. The young mother was spooning food into one infant's mouth, while another one bawled, and the other one just sat in his high chair looking stunned, or perhaps, demented. The trashy mother was wearing a skin-tight top and a short skirt that made her look like a whore. Perhaps she was the town slut, and each of these children was from a different father. The man she was with—her husband?—might not be the father of any of the kids. He would have been handsome had his face not been hideously pocked. Muriel wondered what he did for a living. What did anyone do for a living in this town? What would her life have been like if she had lived it all here?

All the people in the restaurant had the burden of earning a living in this town, many after moving halfway around the world in pursuit of the American dream. Muriel had spent her whole life thinking she had to be something to somebody. But what she was now was so much better. Unlike all these people, Muriel and Wilbur would be leaving this town tomorrow. They were just passing through. They were strangers.

Chapter Twenty-one

Flora was riding up Highway 101 from Santa Barbara with Jonah when she thought to call home and retrieve the messages from their machine. She couldn't remember when she had last heard from her mother. This was what it would be like when her mother was dead, she thought. It would be like she was on an endless road trip with a tall silent stranger having the time of her life, and Flora wouldn't have to be devastated with grief. It could actually be that the real purpose of her mother's trip was one that was noble and altruistic, occasioned by Muriel's supreme mothering instinct which told her to prepare Flora for the inevitable—for the day when she would no longer be coming home. This could be the real purpose of this trip, Flora thought, even if Muriel was completely unaware of it.

Jonah had just finished giving a talk at a synagogue in Santa Barbara, and Flora had gone with him, since they would only be gone for the weekend and she could be back in time to teach her classes on Tuesday. When she checked her messages she found that yes, her mother had called. She had become just an airy voice on the phone.

"Should we stop at the butterfly preserve?" Jonah asked. Their host in Santa Barbara had said it was not to be missed.

"Do you remember the exit he said to take?" she answered.

"It's Annie Glen. Look for the sign. Did you see that?"

"What?" she asked, putting her phone back in her purse.

"That sign."

"What sign?"

"That sign that looked like one of those signs that say 'This stretch of highway was adopted by so and so . . .'"

"No, what did it say?"

"It said, 'Ghosts are everywhere.'"

"Ghosts are everywhere?" she asked.

"That's what it said," Jonah said.

"How could that be a sign on the highway? Could it be the name of a place? Is it a joke? Is it an ad?" Flora wondered.

Then Jonah said, "There it is. There's the Annie Glen exit sign."

Soon they were riding through a development of dilapidated working-class ranch houses built in the sixties, probably, Flora guessed. They were all lined up facing each other on either side of a treeless street with sidewalks separating their front yards from the strips of lawn which bordered the curb. They had garages filled with paint cans and lawn mowers, and some of the driveways had boats or camper tops resting on them. Inside the houses there would be shag rugs and avocado-colored refrigerators and beamed ceilings and family pets and beer bottles and empty buckets from KFC. The butterfly preserve was at the end of this street which was a cul-de-sac. Somehow Flora had assumed the path into the butterfly preserve would be in some wild, national park-like place. There was something eerie about this street, though the lawns were emerald green and the sky above the dilapidated houses was a sapphire blue. Who would she be and what would her life be like if she lived on this street?

Jonah pulled over to the curb close to the end of the block and the entrance to the butterfly preserve. He locked the car, and they made their way past a swinging white metal barrier onto a hillside of eucalyptus with clay soil upon which no grass grew. The ground was light brown, smooth and dully shining, and all was in shadow. Coming toward Flora and Jonah were what must have been two denizens of the neighborhood—a big white man in shorts and a white wife-beater tee-shirt with a tiny dog on a leash, followed by a tiny pale girl with a huge German shepherd on the end of her leash, pulling her along. But it wasn't the big dog with the small girl or the small dog with the big man that was so startling to Flora. It was the pale little girl's eyes—they were too big and too wide for her face.

130

Flora looked away. She had imagined that the butterfly preserve would be in sparkling sunshine, but the eucalyptus trees cast a profound shadow. Next on the trail, Flora and Jonah encountered a middle-aged woman walking an overweight golden retriever, also on a leash. The old dog labored along, stumbling into roots that projected onto the path. Every golden retriever Flora saw made her think of her dead golden retriever. She missed him, his soul, which was so full it comforted whoever was near. She wondered where he was, if he was a ghost. "Ghosts are everywhere," the sign had said. This was a proposition she had never taken seriously before.

Suddenly Flora saw her first butterflies. They were in the middle of the clay path. One was on top of the other, and they were jerking around a bit. They were making love. Was this why butterflies came here? Jonah was getting ahead of her while she gawked at this sight. So she left the scene, following Jonah forward. Straight ahead of her, through the trees, she saw that a semicircle of people had gathered. They were standing and gazing into the trees in front of them, across a gully. The trees were filled with butterflies, moving their wings slowly back and forth.

This sight was slightly disgusting to Flora. It was actually like being around a bunch of fluttering insects. Everyone was taking pictures with their camera phones. Flora felt that she should take a picture with her camera phone. She considered going back down the trail to look for those butterflies that were screwing. They were on the ground, and if they were still going at it, she would be able to get a good shot of them. She wanted to leave, anyway.

So did Jonah, so they turned and walked down the trail again. Did things like the butterflies actually lay eggs in the land of the dead? Could you still have sex after you died? But wouldn't that be sick sex? Was that what Dante was all about? And those Bosch paintings? And everything always in shadow. Flora was fooling herself. It was all wishful thinking. Her mother wasn't protecting her! Her expiration date was still in force. This visit to the butterfly preserve was a foretaste of what was coming, across the River Styx.

Chapter Twenty-two

At the motel, Wilbur's jumpsuit was hanging in the open closet on the rod provided for the convenience of the guests. Wilbur himself was sitting in his white cotton boxer shorts and his white cotton tee-shirt, both made in America, in front of the TV. He was watching Jay Leno. This was the only program he watched besides the *O'Reilly Factor*. He was doing his email at the same time, corresponding with other bridge players, people Muriel didn't know. She had just washed her face and brushed her teeth. She was wearing her white cotton nightgown. She went over to the door, to make sure that it was locked before turning off the light in the hall. There was a sign on the back of the door she hadn't noticed earlier titled GUEST ROOM SECURITY.

FOR ADDITIONAL SECURITY, UTILIZE THE DEAD BOLT . . .

Was the level of security one needed a matter of discretion? Was it optional to have the additional layer of security? Security from what? From marauding bands? She debated whether to turn the deadbolt. With Wilbur, she felt no particular need for extra security. Without him, she would have turned the lock without thinking—and why was it called a dead bolt, she wondered? But she knew why. It was named after the sound the bolt made falling into place—a final sound, a sound which heralded the end of all movement.

Muriel read further: . . . AND SECURE THE WINDOWS AND SLIDING GLASS DOORS . . . Muriel had opened the window to look at the jackrabbit, and she hadn't closed it. There was no sliding glass door, so at least she hadn't blown that part of the instructions.

AS AN ADDITIONAL PRECAUTION, PLEASE SECURE THE SAFETY CHAIN LOCK AND KEEP YOUR WINDOWS CLOSED AND LOCKED. Here an even higher level of security was offered. Muriel slipped on the chain. She wasn't going to take any chances. She didn't know where they were or the level of violence and chaos ready to erupt in the environs.

DO NOT ADMIT PERSONS TO YOUR ROOM WITHOUT FIRST MAKING IDEN-TIFICATION. A ONE-WAY VIEWER IS PROVIDED IN YOUR DOOR FOR YOUR CON-VENIENCE. Yes, there were people out there who knocked on motel room doors and said "Housekeeping," and when you opened the door to them, they came in and shut it behind them, and they turned the dead bolt and put on the chain, and then they pinned you to the bed, and their accomplice cut out your tongue.

IF THERE IS ANY DOUBT ABOUT A PERSON'S TRUE IDENTITY, PLEASE CON-TACT THE FRONT DESK, the security guide concluded. Muriel looked over at Wilbur, sitting in front of the TV, his large face with its nose slightly to one side, as if a mule had kicked it, impassive. She didn't have any doubt about his true identity.

He was exactly what he looked like. It was she who was not.

Chapter Twenty-three

Flora was reading a compelling passage describing the crossing of the River Styx:

> As each wave overtakes us, we're sharply lifted up its slope, then we stare down into the trough as the boat surges ahead. We balance for a moment on the wave's crest, and as we drop almost weightlessly into the following trough, we glance behind to see how big the next wave is going to be. I couldn't guess the height of these waves. All I know is that we vanish behind them, that water swallows up the horizon, and that the ocean seems to draw us down inside itself. There is no chance to think, nor any reason to bother.

This was not literally about the River Styx, of course. It was a description of trying to land a fishing boat on a small island in Alaska's Inside Passage, a place Flora had visited the previous summer on a sea-kayaking trip with Jonah. The tiny islands they had paddled to were so heavenly that, ever since, she had been returning there in her imagination. She kept *The Island Within* by Richard Nelson, a book which richly described this region, by her side of the bed; and she had been dipping into it all morning —trying to distract herself from the thought of her expiration date—when she came across the passage.

FLORA SOMETIMES went with Jonah when he made pastoral visits to the sick and the dying, on those occasions when she had a particular relationship with the person. Today Jonah was going to visit an elderly man who'd had a stroke, and then another elderly man who was on his deathbed. Both were congregants. He had cared for everyone in their families, guiding them through each and every life cycle event, crisis, and joy for the past fifteen years. So to these people he was bound, as a parent to a child. Flora also had an affectionate relationship with each of these particular men, so she went with Jonah to the hospital.

Irwin, the man who'd had the stroke, was almost a cousin, in fact. His first wife, who had died in childbirth, had been Muriel's first cousin. His second wife, the stepmother to his children, had died the year before. Now he was on his third wife, a woman not much older than Flora. Why did so many men prefer to be with young women? Was it because looking into the face of an old woman every day would be too much like looking into a mirror, too much of a reminder that their days were numbered? And why did certain young women prefer to be married to men who were much older than they were? Was it because they felt wonderfully young, wonderfully distant from death when they were with an old person, because, by comparison, they were?

Irwin was always very friendly to Flora when he saw her at the synagogue. He would always ask after Muriel, his cousin, and then he would ask how old Muriel was, even though Flora had told him many times: Muriel was two years older than Irwin. He seemed to gloat about this. He wasn't the oldest mummy left on the planet—no, Muriel was older than he was. It seemed to Flora that he thought if he could point out that there was actually someone older than he was then he wouldn't be at the end of the line. This was all just speculation on Flora's part, of course. She had no idea what went on in his head.

She followed Jonah from the parking lot to the lobby to the elevator, to Irwin's room. Jonah went up to the bed and greeted Irwin, and Irwin replied in pure gibberish. The stroke had apparently affected his speech. To Flora, the horror of this scene was that he seemed aware that he was failing to make himself understood. He motioned for a pencil, and Jonah handed it to him. Flora reached into her bag and found her notebook. She opened it to a blank page, and handed it to Irwin, who wrote on it furiously. Then he handed the notebook back to Jonah. Flora read what Irwin had written. At least, she tried to read it. It was an indecipherable succession of letters and symbols. It looked like the language her computer sometimes printed out, a message from another dimension.

What was the dimension of the dead?

There was another passage in *The Island Within* which had caught her eye this morning, a Koyukon riddle:

> *Wait, I see something: It sounds like a lullaby is being sung to children in the other world.*
> *Answer: The sound of swiftly moving water.*

Flora loved this riddle. It made the other world sound comforting and appealing. It said that after you die, your experience will be equivalent to hearing the sound of swiftly moving water, a wonderful sound, a sound which fills you with excitement. Since the Koyukon were an ancient people, there was every reason to hope that their idea of the next world was accurate. The next world didn't necessarily have to be like the fluttery butterfly preserve.

Next Jonah led Flora to another wing of the hospital where Marcel was dying. His beloved wife Zelda, who had been half his age, had died just a year ago. She was younger, she wasn't supposed to die first. Now Zelda's three best friends were gathered around Marcel's deathbed, massaging him. One of the women was doing his feet. "Don't stop doing my feet," he said to her, weakly. This amazed Flora—that one could experience physical pleasure as one was dying, that the body would feel and respond to touch up until the very end. And she thought of how people became more and more isolated as they aged and were touched less and less; and she remembered her mother telling her how she and Wilbur hugged, and how happy she had sounded when she said this.

Another of the women was rubbing Marcel's chest. "Open my gown," he said to her. "Put your hands right on my skin. Use oil."

Again, Flora was impressed. Why did people usually just stand by the bed of the dying, she thought? Clearly, the dying wanted to be touched. Clearly, human touch was a fundamental desire, which lasted right up to the very onset of death. Gratitude filled her heart that she had Jonah to go to sleep next to every night.

"There's too much light in here," Marcel breathed, and one of the women turned down the light.

"He started complaining about the light an hour ago," the woman said. "Is the light hurting your eyes?"

"It's not allowing me to die fast enough," he said. "I want to get to Zelda!"

There it was again, the belief that when you died you could reunite with your dead loved ones. It was such a widespread belief, and when the dying subscribed to it, it leant the idea credibility. After all, one might expect those standing on the threshold to have a better view into the beyond than those standing behind them, those still in the midst of life. Flora, of course, wished that it might be true, but she knew it was only a wish, a powerful wish, and there was no way to know for sure about anything that happened after death, except that the body rotted away and returned to the earth.

"Marcel," Jonah said. "Would you like me to say the *vidui* for you? The *vidui* was the confession Jews were supposed to make on their deathbeds, which a rabbi could say for them if they were too infirm.

"Yes, please, Rabbi," Marcel said.

So Jonah read the confession to him in Hebrew, while the women continued massaging him and Flora watched from the sidelines. Then he repeated what he had just said, in English:

O Lord our God and God of our Fathers, we acknowledge that our life is in your hands. May it be your will that you send perfect healing to Marcel. Yet if it is your final decree that he be taken by death, let it be in love. May his death atone for the sins and transgressions which he committed before You. Grant him of the abundant good which is held in store for the righteous, and give him life replete with joy in Your Presence, at Your right hand forever.

How was it that death atoned for our sins, Flora wondered? Was it somehow a final righting of the balance? How futilely she had argued for her own life in the cosmic courtroom, protesting the injustice of her sentence. Who was she to think she could comprehend or assess divine justice?

Maybe the next world was more like a tiny island in Alaska's Haida Strait than a butterfly preserve. Flora returned to this island in her imagination once again, hearing the lapping of the waves on the beach as they paddled their boat into shore, and the sight of the little geysers of water shooting out of clams in the sand, small dear replicas of the whales' spouting behind them in the strait. As they pulled their boat up on the rocks, the sea churned with life all around the island. Otters floated on their backs, salmon leapt, jellyfish floated, and sea urchins waved. Overhead, the sky was an all-encompassing grey, and the air was temperate. They made their way into the interior of the island. Beneath their feet the ground was a thick spongy loam, and soon they were in a dense forest of Sitka spruce. Some trees were very old and very tall, some just fallen over, and others long into decay. Each tree, in each stage of growing or decay was necessary to the balance of the whole. Everything was working in harmony. What was so wonderful about it was that there was nothing extra here, no waste. It sustained all life. That's why Flora thought it might be heaven.

Jonah took Flora's arm. They left Marcel's room, went down on the elevator, out through the lobby, and into the day.

Chapter Twenty-four

Muriel and Wilbur were in the middle of a hailstorm, one of the most violent hailstorms of the century, on the highway between New Mexico and Texas. That was just how it was going to be from hereon in: everything was going to be more violent and extreme. Not like it was when Muriel was a child, when weather was always regular and predictable, and stayed within certain boundaries. The world was ending, and it was interesting to be here right at the end. She was sorry to witness the end of the world unfolding, but she was glad to know for sure that it was true: nothing lasts.

The hail pounded on the roof of the Dodge and bounced off the windshield. The sky had suddenly gotten dark. Wilbur drove with his face straight ahead, cradling the wheel, never glancing over at Muriel. He was going to dump her. He was going to look her up on the Internet. He was going to find out how old she was, and he was going to dump her.

She should dump him first, he was so boring. He never spoke. All he did was get up early in the morning and work on his bridge system. Whatever she said, he would answer, "Yes, I guess." They would go to McDonald's, and he would have an egg muffin thing; and then they would go to play bridge, and he would be trying as hard as he could to win points, because if he did, it would prove the efficacy of his system. Muriel was trying as hard as she could to learn his system, but she couldn't remember it all, and she kept messing up. She knew he was getting angry with her, although he wouldn't say anything. He was trying to get her to say something, to make it easier for him to dump her, she thought.

The place where they had stayed in New Mexico had been the site of an early nuclear explosion. It was a completely desolate landscape. There they stayed in the officers' quarters at an air force base, which gave Muriel a chance to do her laundry. She was standing and watching it go around and around in the dryer when Wilbur came running in and told her that her purse was ringing. He was carrying it. She reached in and answered the phone. It was Flora. She wanted to know if Muriel was all right. Wilbur was standing right there. "I can't really say," she said.

"Mom, are you being held hostage? Does he have a gun to your head?"

"I wouldn't put it that way," Muriel said, as Wilbur left to go back to their room. "I just can't explain it," she said to Flora. "Of course, it's all about bridge. That's all he's interested in."

"That's all you're interested in," Flora said.

"But I'm not very good at it. He's going to dump me for a better bridge player. He's been emailing back and forth with this professor from Ohio. They're making plans to play with each other at the tournament in Colorado. What am I supposed to do?"

"I don't know, Mom."

There had been nothing to do in that little town in New Mexico. Muriel made Wilbur go out for a walk. He didn't want to. He wanted to sit and nurse a Dr. Pepper at the Burger King. But she made him, though the heat was intense in the middle of the day, and clouds of radioactive dust rose around their feet. He was completely out of breath, while she wasn't, and she was fourteen years older.

Later, she checked out a book from the little library at the base. It was based on a popular TV show where you were offered two wishes. What were her two wishes? One would be that Wilbur never found out how old she was. Actually, she could wish she wasn't as old as she was. Did she want to be young again? One day when they were out walking on Crissy Field, Flora had asked Muriel what she thought was the best time of her life. "I don't know," she had told her.

"Could it be now?" Flora asked.

"Maybe it is," she said. She couldn't really remember anything before now, anyway.

Muriel had to muster all her self-control to bite back her tongue and not tell Wilbur how boring it was to be with him. The sound of the hail pounding on the roof was deafening. How could he drive through this? And where was he taking her?

Into Texas. Deep into Texas. So deep into Texas she might never come out.

Chapter Twenty-five

Flora could tell from the caller ID on her phone that it was her mother.

"Mom, where are you?" she asked.

"I'm in Texas, Kerrville, Texas," Muriel answered. "I'm coming back. If I can get to the airport."

"What do you mean if you can get to the airport?"

"Wilbur dumped me! Just as I told you he would."

"What do you mean? How did it happen? Are you okay?"

"I think so. He said he would drive me to the airport. I guess he's anxious to get rid of me so he can play with that professor who's been learning his system. So I'm out in the cold now because I couldn't learn his stupid system. He was making me so nervous I couldn't think."

"So he didn't get rid of you because he found out your age?"

"Well, he might have. He didn't say anything about it. He just said he wanted to be happy, and he thought I should leave."

"Just out of the blue, apropos of nothing?" Flora asked.

"Well, not exactly," Muriel admitted. "It was because of something I said."

"Uh oh," Flora said.

"It must be because he's such a Southern Baptist."

"What did you say?" Flora asked.

"I kept trying, but I couldn't learn his system. He was making me so uptight, and I just lost it. I said, 'I don't give a—you know.'"

"You think it was because you said 'shit'? He couldn't take it that you said 'shit'?"

"He's a Southern Baptist. I don't know, maybe it was just an excuse. Now I have to come back. You're going to have to put up with me again."

"Mom, I want to see you."

"I'll call you when I get back, if it's not too much of a burden for you. I know how busy you are."

Flora put down the phone. Her mother had sounded sarcastic. She was angry, and when her mother was angry, she could get nasty.

"What happened?" Jonah asked, sitting up in bed next to Flora.

"There goes my theory that Wilbur was her heavenly reward for standing between me and *It*," Flora said.

"So you really think there are heavenly rewards?" Jonah said.

"Don't you? You're the rabbi."

"Well just because I'm a rabbi doesn't mean I'm an idiot. I have no idea if there are heavenly rewards and punishments or not, but even if there are, how could we presume to know what is a reward and what isn't, and what the reward is for and what it's not?"

"So Wilbur could have been a reward to Muriel for something that had nothing at all to do with me?" Flora asked.

"Exactly," Jonah said, looking at Flora in the mirror on the closet doors opposite the bed.

"Wilbur might actually have been a punishment, and not a reward at all?"

"Or neither," Jonah said.

"It's a little scary to think how we just go through our lives assuming we understand how everything works, when actually we don't have a clue," Flora said.

"Well, we do have a clue," Jonah said. "This feeling in the gut that virtue is somehow rewarded even if it doesn't seem to be in this world."

In the mirror Flora was seeing her smooth white limbs entwined with his dark hairy ones. They looked like different species, and yet they were so alike! It was a miracle. Perhaps it was only being in love that made her think that the world made sense, that justice and compassion ruled heaven and earth.

"Nobody else understands me but you," Flora said.

"I don't understand anybody else," Jonah said.

Flora wondered what her mother needed for life to seem meaningful to her. The mystery of other people's lives, how they lived in response to what they believed gave life meaning, produced great awe in Flora. The mystery that there was such a thing as a life at all bowled her over.

She herself had had more than her fair share of joy in the course of her life—from her chosen work, and from her husband and her daughters. Lately, she had even had some measure of joy from her relationship with her mother. Her expiration date could come to pass, and she could leave this mortal coil with gratitude in her heart. Or she thought she could. Her mother, on the other hand, clearly had not reached that place. There was something else which needed to happen before she'd be ready to let go. That might, in fact, explain her longevity, and why Wilbur couldn't be the final act, her final reward. Apparently, Muriel still had miles to go before she slept.

Chapter Twenty-six

There had been this large lump in Muriel's left forearm. She knew she should go to the doctor to get it checked out, but she didn't. She didn't have time. Since returning to Laurel Dell she had been busy every day of the week, with bridge dates in Laurel Dell as well as Oakland. She had called all her old partners to make dates, while waiting for the plane to take off in Texas. She was also busy going on the walks sponsored by the Laurel Dell Bird Watcher's Club, volunteering at the Computer Club, and going to the meetings of the Great Books Club, the Mystery Book Club, and the Current Events Discussion Group held at the Jewish Community Center just outside the gates of Laurel Dell. She had to go to her appointment with the personal trainer at the Laurel Dell gym—three such appointments were included in her Laurel Dell dues—and she was also busy attending the dances which featured a live band once a month in one of the clubhouses. But when she came home after all of this, she still had to have dinner alone; and even if she went out to dinner with other people, she still had to come home to an empty house.

She had been talked into going to the dances by one of her bridge partners, a man named Irving, who was Chinese and no bigger than a minute. She had protested to him that she hadn't danced in years, and he told her that it wasn't a problem. So she put on a pair of pantyhose and a skirt, and drove down to the clubhouse where Irving was waiting for her in a neat little suit, and as it turned out, she danced pretty well, and it was fun. While she was at the dance, she wasn't thinking about the lump that was growing in her arm or feeling she should be doing something about it. She didn't trust the doctors here at the clinic next to Laurel Dell, so she wasn't sure how she was going to get it looked at. She just postponed worrying about it. After all, she was old. She could just die. What was the point of any of it, anyway? Though the point of it all eluded her, she still felt an intense urge to live, just to be alive, nonetheless. And she was fueled by the desire to see everything and to do everything.

Also, Muriel did not want to give up her shape. Once she gave that up, it would be the end. She would rather lose her mind than her shape. And even though Wilbur had dumped her, she wasn't going to give him the satisfaction of just curling up in a ball and giving up. So she kept her calendar full.

She went to the movies in the Laurel Dell theater with Pauline. It was a beautiful theater, and it was free. Only it was filled with women, women saving seats for other women, and hardly any men. She had been having trouble hearing what they said in the movies, though. Nobody knew how to enunciate anymore.

Daphne had been after her to get a hearing aid, and she did finally go and get one just to get Daphne to stop nagging her—but she didn't always wear it. She hadn't wanted to get one because she was afraid it would make her look old. She had been able to get one which hardly showed, but she wasn't sure it made things any better. Now when she was in a restaurant, she heard the background noise of dishes clattering, and that was annoying. She only wanted to hear what she wanted to hear, what the actors were saying in the movies and what her friends were saying when she was out to dinner with them.

She had a date to go out to dinner with Pierre—Dutch treat, of course. As she was getting dressed and pulling her hand through the sleeve of her sweater, she saw the lump on her arm. She promised herself she would get it looked at soon. While she was dressing, the woman who lived upstairs was dying. As Muriel was walking out to her car, she saw the ambulance parked in front, and the stretcher carrying the woman out, and she knew that she was dead. She and her husband were nice people and good neighbors. They collected Muriel's mail for her when she was out of town, and she had taken them both out to dinner as a thank-you. Now she was glad that she had.

146

After a few days, Muriel went upstairs and rang the bell to see how her neighbor was doing. They had been a devoted couple. Her newly minted widower neighbor opened the door. He was drinking wine by himself. He invited Muriel in for a glass.

There was that joke commonly told in Laurel Dell, that as soon as a woman died, the widowed man's doorbell would ring and there would be dozens of women outside with casseroles. Muriel noticed some on the counter as she took the glass of wine her neighbor proffered. The wine was good. She was worried that he was depressed. He seemed glad to have her company.

After all, who else but another widowed person could understand how terrible it was to sit alone in one's house? Living alone was hardly like being alive at all. The dead wife was his second; they had been together twenty years, and they had been happy. He wasn't interested in shaking his depression now, it seemed to Muriel. But the following week, at his suggestion, they went out to dinner at a place in Walnut Creek that had just opened and was pretty swanky. It was called the Bistro. She had a martini, and so did he. But after that night she didn't see him. She was always gone, out and about, coming home late, leaving home early, and she didn't run into him. He didn't call her, and she didn't call him. Finally, one night she did call him up, just to make sure he was okay—that he hadn't shot himself alone upstairs in his condo—and he was all right. He had been asleep, though it was only 8:00.

Muriel made plans—to drive to Los Angeles to see her friends there, to play at her old bridge club, and also to go to her old dermatologist who would burn off every brown mark on her face graciously, never questioning whether she should bother treating a woman who was so old. She could ask her old dermatologist about the lump in her arm. She might know what it was and what Muriel should do about it. She promised herself that she would, and then she made plans to go to Denver for the tournament, even though she might run into Wilbur there. She practiced what she would say if she saw him.

Fred had invited her to stay at his condo again, and Justine wasn't coming this time. She didn't think Fred had ever found out about her relationship with Wilbur, so she would not have to feel any embarrassment about it. She would go to a doctor after she got back from Denver. That was her plan.

Anyway, the lump in her arm was probably a lipoma, a harmless fatty tumor, benign. She'd had just such a tumor in her other forearm, almost twenty-five years ago. She knew it was twenty-five years ago because she remembered she had first noticed it when Flora was pregnant with Lulu, and Flora had told her recently that Lulu was almost twenty-five. How could she have such old grandchildren? A lot of her neighbors had little grandchildren, they were always babysitting for them; and when they showed her their pictures that they always carried Muriel would coo, but she wasn't really interested. This lump on the other arm, her left arm, was probably a fatty tumor like the first one. But what if it wasn't? What if it was a virulent cancer which was devouring her arm and making it look fat, a tumor which would very soon take over all her inner organs and tissues, turning them black?

Muriel now signed up for every Laurel Dell outing that she could, even when she didn't have anyone to go with. People were friendly, and it didn't matter that she didn't have anyone to sit with on the bus. Nice people chatted with her. So she saw the Petaluma River, a beautiful garden she had never heard of before down on the peninsula, and a Broadway show in San Francisco. She went on a Napa Valley wine tour, to a Monet exhibit at the Palace of the Legion of Honor; and she had brunch at a beautiful restaurant in the village of Capitola, near where her granddaughter Posey went to college at U.C. Santa Cruz.

She took the Laurel Dell bus to Carmel, where she met two old friends she had never lost touch with from the days when Jack was in business—that's how they met, through Jack's business. When these friends had retired and moved from the valley to Pacific Grove to be closer to their children, Muriel and Jack had stayed in touch and visited them at their new house. And then when she and Jack had moved north, Muriel had discovered that once a month there was a Laurel Dell bus trip to Carmel, and she started taking it so that even though Jack couldn't go, she could keep up her friendship with these friends, Dorothy and Jim. Jim had had a stroke and was in a wheelchair, but Dorothy would drive to Carmel to meet Muriel, and they would sit and have lunch. But at the end of each day, her rooms stretched around her, all empty. She was still alone, and there was this huge lump in her arm.

Chapter Twenty-seven

When her mother got into the passenger seat of her car, she picked up a nickel that was on the floor by her feet. "No one bothers to pick up a nickel anymore, I see," she said.

Flora felt attacked—and found out. Muriel now had proof that Flora was just as careless of money as if it grew on trees—as if she had any to waste. Had Flora been a better person, she never would have wasted a penny, and then she'd have plenty. Muriel had gone through the Depression, and that was why she was so careful, she had explained on numerous occasions, adding that her daughters, on the other hand, had been spoiled.

Flora, for her part, did not believe that children could be spoiled. She thought that was a myth from her mother's generation, along with the myth of the nymphomaniac—which was premised on the idea that a woman who liked sex was a monster—along with the myth that when bad things happened to you, it was your own fault. She felt her mother's eye on her, judging her. But she also knew her mother needed to attack her, to relieve some of the pent-up anger she was carrying around. Muriel had been in a nasty mood ever since she got back from Texas.

This morning, Flora had driven to Walnut Creek to take Muriel to the doctor's office for her biopsy, in case she was not feeling well enough afterwards to drive herself home. They were early, so they parked in the parking lot by some rose bushes, laden with full blooms. Muriel sat cursing the hospital across the boulevard. "I don't like coming to a doctor's office so close to that damn hospital," she said. "That's the damn hospital where everybody dies. What if I need surgery? This doctor is probably attached to that damn hospital! I'm not going into it."

"Mom, don't be ridiculous," Flora said, and they walked through the parking lot and up the stairs to the office.

Muriel stopped to read the nameplates outside the door. "So many doctors in one office!" she said, disapprovingly. Then they went inside, and Muriel announced to the receptionist that she was there. "Take a seat," the woman said, from behind her little window. "The doctor will call you in soon."

"Why does the doctor only schedule procedures on Friday?" Muriel asked. She was annoyed, Flora knew, because she had to miss her regular Friday bridge date to come for the biopsy.

"Because he only has the use of the room where they do the procedures on Fridays," the nurse said.

"Is that because there are so many other names on the door, and every name on the door has to share this one room for procedures?" Muriel asked.

"Mother, please," Flora said, and Muriel sat down. Flora pitied the doctor. Her mother was in a rage.

In a little while, they called Muriel in, and Flora followed her into the room where the procedure was to take place. They put her mother in a big reclining chair with a tray for her arm to rest on. She looked apprehensive. "Don't hurt me," she said. The doctor was fat with a head of black hair and a black beard, just as Muriel had described him to Flora. The room was a horrifying green, and silver instruments gleamed on the trays. The nurse came into the room to assist, and the doctor told Flora she had to leave, that there wasn't enough room for her to stay—the room was too small. So she went out to sit in the waiting room.

She felt a bit of panic. What were they going to do to her mother? Were they going to hurt her? The biopsy was for this large lump. It didn't look good. But she had had such a lump before, and it had turned out to be harmless. She remembered that it was around the same time that Flora's expiration date was handed down to her, almost twenty-five years ago. Now that date was looming just over the horizon. This lump was a bookend.

Flora was almost positive that it was benign, but what if it was deadly, a lump that was going to kill her mother, and then, by extension, kill Flora, once her mother wasn't there anymore to protect her?

Yet what if her mother had never been driven by a maternal instinct to protect her? What if that was merely Flora's fantasy, born out of the jealous need of a baby to have her mother's life devoted to her own? What if Muriel was only trying to protect herself all along? What if she was simply a fierce and vital creature who was very good at fighting for her own survival, with no thought at all about the survival of her daughter?

On the other hand, what if Flora was the one protecting Muriel from *her* expiration date? What if Flora was going to live past her sixtieth birthday just so she could be there for her mother? Perhaps these things worked both ways.

The door opened, and the nurse told Flora she could come in now. Her mother was lying back in the big chair with her arm on a tray looking terrified and fulminating with anger. The doctor was saying, "I don't know why it hurt you. I didn't think it would have hurt so much, because the needle would just be going through fat. But it had to go through tissue and sinew which I hadn't expected the tumor to be made of."

"Mother, are you all right?" Flora said.

"I'm in pain," she said.

"I can write you a prescription for Vicodin, Mrs. Margolin," the doctor said.

"I don't want Vicodin," Muriel said.

"She won't fill the prescription," Flora said. She was proud of her mother for having the fortitude to endure what other people were too weak to. But she also found her mother's disdain for anyone who didn't have her self-control a little frightening.

"Can you stand up without feeling dizzy? Let's give it a try," the doctor said.

Flora took Muriel's good arm to help her stand up, and they walked through the door.

"The doctor wanted you to have this," the nurse said, handing a slip of paper to Muriel.

It was the prescription for Vicodin. Flora took it, and they made it down the steps to the parking lot. There, Muriel approached a little Mercedes that resembled her own with her key in her hand, and tried to beep it open.

"Mom, we came in my car, and we parked over there, by the rose bushes," Flora said.

As they drove back to Laurel Dell in Flora's Toyota, Flora could feel Muriel's anger about to boil over. The final indignity to her mother, Flora knew, was having someone else drive her. It meant she had become incapable.

Chapter Twenty-eight

Muriel received an invitation in the mail to come to a tea where they would be serving dessert and inviting people to consider buying a condominium in the Roxbury Arms, the new senior living residence being built in San Francisco. Scheduled to be ready for occupancy within three years, it touted a revolutionary new concept, a twenty-first century advance in elegant senior living. This appealed to Muriel, and she decided to go.

The event was free, at an upscale restaurant in Walnut Creek. About a dozen other people were in attendance. Muriel chose a slice of the chocolate cake, but it was much too big for her. She poured herself some tea before it got too strong. She recognized a few of the people from Laurel Dell. Everyone there was well-off. You had to be well-off to contemplate buying a condominium that started at a million dollars, with four thousand dollars a month dues. It was a very high-class place. That was part of the appeal of the Roxbury—if she moved there, she'd occupy a position in the upper crust. And after all, in three years she might need to give up driving. How old could you be and legally drive? And if she gave up driving, she'd be better off in the city, closer to Flora, who could drive her around the way she had driven her mother. She would be closer to her granddaughters, and maybe she'd really get to know them. By that time, she would be past worrying about them or worrying that they were a disappointment to her. She'd be living in a deluxe new building with a cocktail lounge and a dining room.

Who knew what would happen in the next three years? Old people were eventually supposed to live in these places, weren't they? If they weren't, why else would they build them? She couldn't stay around for the question-and-answer period, unfortunately, because she had to get home. A man from the Computer Club was coming to fix her computer. She couldn't get the Internet anymore. That was one good thing about Laurel Dell—volunteers from the Computer Club would come up to your house there and fix your computer for free.

He was waiting for her outside in his truck when she pulled up. She brought him in and led him to her computer desk. His name was Gene. He just loved helping people in Laurel Dell with their computers. He went all around there fixing people's hardware and software. He had been in a lot of houses, and hers was certainly a nice one, he said. Yes, he had met all sorts of folks. And plenty of lonely widows. He himself was a widower, had been for the last six months. Before that, he'd had a long and faithful marriage. After he retired, he and the wife moved to the mountains, the gold country, where there were plenty of trees and very few people—so far out there, you could drive for miles and miles and never encounter another car on the road. But a few years ago, his wife had gotten sick. She had diabetes and had a stroke. There was no way they could continue to live so far from a hospital. That was when they bought a little condominium down in the flat part of Laurel Dell. He had worked hard as an engineer, and their kids were both quite successful, the two of them that were left. Another one had died of lymphoma when she was only twenty. He had cared for his wife until she died, doing all the cooking and the chores.

Muriel looked at him. He was a lot shorter than any man she had ever been with before, though he was several inches taller than she was. He was slim and wiry, and he had a full head of silver hair. What she liked about him was his smile, and he smiled a lot.

"There was this woman," he went on, "who asked me to come up and look at her computer and see if I could fix it, and I did. And then the next day there's a message waiting for me from her down at the Computer Club, see? She wanted me to come back up to her house—she was way up here on the hill—and take a look at her computer again. Well, gall darn, she kept leaving me messages, every day, and I kept going back up there. But I was getting tuckered out, so I just stopped picking up her messages."

"Oh, really?" Muriel said.

"There was this old couple I visited today—they were having trouble replacing their print cartridge—you know, there's a lot of old people shacking up here at the Wrinkle Ranch, that's what I call it. Anyway, I put that cartridge right in for these old people, and the old woman was so grateful, she gave me a great big hug. She said her husband had tried twenty-seven times to stick it in and couldn't do it once, and I had popped it right in. Okay, Mrs. Margolin, may I call you Muriel? Your Internet is up, you're all set to go. Aren't you going to give me a hug?"

Muriel wasn't sure of what she thought about all this. She allowed him to put his arms around her. "You call that a hug?" he asked, and he laughed, and left.

THE NEXT morning, Muriel pulled out the Laurel Dell directory and called up the Computer Club. A woman answered, a woman Muriel knew from the Bridge Club. She was volunteering, answering phones at the Computer Club. It was a prized position. Muriel had done it herself, briefly, but she had started traveling so much that they took her off their list of volunteers. "I'd like to leave a message for Gene," she said to the woman manning the desk. Was Gene his name? She couldn't remember. She thought it was. "He was up at my place yesterday, fixing my computer, and it still isn't right. I was wondering if you could ask him to call me to schedule another time for him to come up?"

HE WAS there late in the afternoon. "This is my last appointment of the day," he said. "What seems to be wrong with your computer now, young lady?"

"I'm not quite sure," she said. "Come take a look at it."

"It looks fine," he said. "It looks very good."

"You do good work," she said.

"And people are generally appreciative," he said. "I usually get a hug. I get plenty of hugs. But yesterday, you didn't give me a hug."

"Yes, I did," she said.

"You call that a hug?" he asked. "You just stood there, all stiff."

"I'm eighty-six," she said. These words came pouring out of her before she could censor them.

"Oh, thank the Lord," he said. "I was afraid you were too young for me!"

"How old are you?" she asked him.

"I'm eighty-two," he said. He wrapped his arms around her and she hugged him close. They stood there hugging and stroking each other, and it felt delicious.

"I HAVE the feeling we're going to have some adventures," she said after a long while, lying beside him.

"Dentures? Yes, I wear dentures," he said, laughing, and he slipped his arm back around her, pulling her close.

Chapter Twenty-nine

Flora had a date to visit Marta Green, a woman exactly her mother's age, a member of Jonah's congregation whom Flora was particularly fond of. A few years ago, after Marta's husband died, she had moved to the Horowitz Center, a posh senior residence where many people from Jonah's congregation ended up, or passed through on their way back to their lives after a month or two of recuperation from a hip replacement, chemotherapy, or the like. The Horowitz Center had handrails in all the hallways and an elegant dining room. Of course, the majority who entered there never returned home; their homes were sold off, as Marta's had been. The majority who moved into this residence moved down from there to the Alzheimer's wing, or to a facility with a full-time nursing staff, or into a hospital where they disappeared into the ether.

Marta was on the younger side of the average resident. When she ran into Flora at synagogue services, she told Flora how happy she was at the Horowitz Center, how glad she was that she had made the move, and how she wanted Flora to come and see her room. When Flora came to see her room, Marta would take her to lunch. The food at the Horowitz Center was exceptional, she said. Flora and Marta talked about Flora coming for lunch every time they ran into each other. A year passed, and finally one day Marta called Flora to set a date for this to happen at last, and now Flora was on her way.

Flora wanted to get something to bring to Marta, but she wasn't sure what. A plant? No—flowers, she decided. Flowers were a good gift.

Marta's husband, Otto, had been an officer of the synagogue when the Roses first arrived, and Otto and Marta, this gracious couple with a slight German accent, had taken their new rabbi's family under their wing. They were both Holocaust survivors, but they had met in San Francisco after the war. Otto had been in a camp; and though Marta's whole family was taken—her parents, her grandparents, and her little sister—Marta had been hidden in a castle in Belgium while the Holocaust raged all around.

Marta had never learned to drive. Otto drove her wherever she needed to go, and otherwise, she took the bus. They had two children. Their grown son and his wife had lived in Japan for a long time, but a few years ago his company had relocated him back to Denver. When Marta spoke of her son, she never expressed bitterness that he had been so far away, only gratitude that he was back in the country.

Marta and Otto's daughter had died of leukemia in 1975, when she was barely thirteen. Flora had seen a picture of her once, a lovely girl with thick brown braids. Flora did not understand how Marta could have survived everything. She was always kind and pleasant. Flora admired her dignified demeanor. She never displayed any anger, bitterness, or depression, not even now, not even after Otto had died horribly of stomach cancer, abandoning her. Marta was a special person, someone Flora thought she could learn from.

Marta had said she would meet Flora in the lobby, and Flora was surprised not to see Marta. She would have guessed that Marta would have been perfectly on time, indeed, early for their appointment. Marta had, for many years, sent her a card on her birthday, remembering it faithfully. Flora had felt happily remembered when she received these cards. They had made her feel honored in her role as the rabbi's wife. To Flora, they had been examples of Marta's genuine kindness.

Marta's perfect politeness was the mark of her sterling character, and Flora tried to emulate her, for it was in this area of manners that Flora frequently felt deficient. As a rabbi's wife, people were constantly doing things for her, and she often felt overwhelmed by the attentions, and her failures to respond in the most appropriate fashion. Flora, a great admirer of the works of

Jane Austen, knew that one's manners were not simply formalities, but the careful way one showed respect for and sensitivity to the feelings of others.

Flora wished she had been raised with more attention paid to this, but Muriel had had little interest in social niceties, though she often expressed admiration for them. She had commented to Flora about how impressed she was with Trude, the first friend she had made in Laurel Dell. Once when Muriel had had an extra symphony ticket and she had taken Trude, her friend had given her a present afterwards. It was a necklace which Trude had made herself, stringing and knotting the glass beads. "She was a real lady," Muriel said to Flora, more than once.

Trude had once made a comment to Muriel that she frequently repeated to Flora. She said that men who would be going after widows like her were either looking for "a nurse or a purse." And of course, she had no interest in being either. But even though Muriel repeated this sentiment to Flora on several occasions, as if it were the sensible position, she didn't really seem to believe it. She was on her second boyfriend since Flora's father's death. It seemed she had met some sort of computer man. Muriel said she wasn't sure if she liked him—she said he was short, and she wasn't sure if she could like a short man.

"But Mom, you're short," Flora had said.

"I'm five-foot-two," Muriel had answered. "And he has dentures," Muriel had said. She still had all her teeth and was always shocked when she discovered other people didn't.

"I'm having trouble remembering his name," she said. "Is it Gene? I think it's Gene, but I'm not sure. Anyway, I'd like to get together with you, but I'm looking at my calendar, and I'm not sure when we can. I've got so many bridge dates. And Gene—I think that's his name—wants to take me up to the Gold Country to see where he used to live. Anyway, I've got to go. I'll call you."

Flora spotted Marta now making her way haltingly to the lobby. She'd had a knee replacement the year before Otto died, and it seemed to Flora that she must not have fully recovered. She didn't use a cane or a walker as so many of the residents here did, but her gait was hesitating and slow, and Flora felt sad when she saw her.

After Marta greeted her, they went upstairs to her room. She had wanted a one-bedroom apartment, but none had been available when she wanted to move in, so she had settled for a room with a bedroom alcove.

"The light is very nice," Flora said.

"Yes, there's not much of a view," Marta said in her dry way, "but the light is very nice, in the afternoon, especially."

That was what Flora appreciated about Marta—her dry acknowledgement of life's disappointments always balanced with a cheerful recognition of the compensating blessings.

Marta's room was elegantly yet simply furnished with pieces Flora recognized from her house. Everything was tasteful, and the room was filled with flowers.

"It was my birthday yesterday," Marta explained, motioning to the various bouquets. "This one is from Carl and Violet," Marta said, pointing to the largest arrangement with obvious pride. Carl was Marta's son, and Violet was his wife, Flora remembered. Then Marta took Flora's offering of sweet peas, put them in a small vase, and set it on the counter in her kitchenette.

"I guess I've brought coals to Newcastle," Flora said, but how could she have known? Perhaps if she had known when Marta's birthday was, as Marta knew when hers was, she would have realized that her flowers might be redundant. "It does look very nice," Flora said, and it did. "Your room is very pleasant," Flora said. "Was it hard for you to leave your house?"

"Not a bit," Marta said. "I was ready to leave."

Flora wondered about this. That was the house where her daughter had been born and where she had died, thirteen years later. That was the house where her husband had gotten sicker and sicker until he also had died.

"Here is something else I'd like to show you," Marta said, leading Flora into her bedroom alcove and opening an ancient wooden box set out on the dresser. Inside was a picture of a young girl with thick brown hair.

161

"This is my little sister," she said. "She was sent into hiding the same as I was, but she got homesick for my parents and went home. I never saw her again."

"The Nazis got her?" Flora asked. "How did you get this picture?"

"A cousin had it, a cousin who was able to get out in time."

All this had happened so long ago, and yet, for Marta it was still part of the world she was living in. Marta had the grace to inhabit this world and at the same time not lose touch with the past, with those who were gone. Her honoring of them and her love for them kept them alive in some deep and simple way that was to Flora pitch-perfect. There was nothing sentimental about Marta; she had true sentiment, something, in Flora's experience, few could manage.

They went down to lunch. The tables were set with white linen tablecloths and napkins, and the glassware sparkled. At all the tables there were bent-over white heads with walkers and electric wheelchairs nearby.

A little white-haired woman waved at Flora from across the room. It was Fritzi, another of Jonah's congregants. Flora had recently been invited to her ninetieth birthday party. But Flora hadn't gone because she'd had plans to go to the symphony with her mother that day. Jonah went, and later Fritzi called to thank Flora for letting him.

"I had nothing to do with it," she protested. "I would have come too, if I hadn't had plans with my mother."

"You know, I'm in love with your husband," Fritzi said, chuckling. If you were ninety, you were allowed to say you were in love with another woman's husband, apparently.

"Now she spotted us," Marta said. "She's going to come over here in a minute and ask me why I didn't tell her you were coming."

"So you like it here? There are activities for you to do?" Flora said.

"Yes, plenty," Marta answered. "I go to the jewelry-making class. I made this necklace myself," she said. "Carl's wife, Violet, sent me these beads. I couldn't ask for a better daughter-in-law than Violet," she said. "I also serve on several committees. This afternoon I have to go to a meeting of the Hospitality Committee."

"How is the hospitality here?" Flora asked.

"It could be better," Marta said. "When I first came, I went down to eat and sat down at a table, and the people there said that seat was taken. So I went to another table, and the people sitting there told me the same thing. That happened four times until I found a place to sit. But now I have my regular table, and everything is fine."

That sounded dreadful to Flora. She promised herself again that she would never allow her mother to move into a place like this. She shuddered, thinking of Marta having to endure this indignity on top of everything else she'd had to suffer in her life. And yet Marta spoke of it without bitterness.

The young waitress brought the food. Flora had ordered a turkey sandwich on rye. She was interested to see that though the turkey was piled high inside the bread, she was served only half a sandwich. Apparently, her mother wasn't the only person who believed one should never eat more than half a sandwich. Here, that idea had been institutionalized.

Flora found herself getting a headache before the meal was over. But before she could make her excuses and leave, Fritzi had maneuvered her walker over to the table where Marta and Flora were sitting.

"Why didn't you tell me she was coming?" Fritzi reprimanded Marta. "Why don't you come upstairs now and I'll show you my room," she commanded both of them.

They had no choice but to follow her. Fritzi's room was decorated with lace curtains and plush furniture. She had something that she wanted to give to Flora for the rabbi. It was a needlepoint she had done of a Hanukah lamp, its eight flames glowing, put into a wooden picture frame. Flora accepted it with as much grace as she could muster. She didn't know what they would do with it. Over the years, congregants had given Jonah many things like this.

Fritzi's phone rang, and Marta and Flora stood there while she sat in front of her computer and embarked upon a long conversation about a bill she had gotten which she was contesting. Finally, Flora and Marta signaled to her that they were leaving, and made their way out the door.

Back in Marta's apartment, she showed Flora a picture of her dead daughter, lifting it carefully from the same ancient ornate box where her sister's photograph came from. The two girls looked quite alike. Their thick brown hair was neatly braided and their round eyes looked out of the pictures calmly, under brows unruffled by the horrors which were about to descend upon them. Flora gazed upon these pure faces, faces which had never aged. These were two young girls whose families' love for them had never been sullied. Then Marta had carefully put the photograph back into the box and closed it.

As Flora put the needlepoint in her car, she noticed there was some writing on the brown paper on the back of the frame. "Happy Mother's Day to my loving mother," it said, and it was signed with Fritzi's daughter's name, and the year, 1975. Clearly Fritzi's daughter had had the needlepoint framed as a Mother's Day present in 1975, but Fritzi wasn't sentimental about this token of her daughter's affection.

Chapter Thirty

Muriel sat gazing at a picture of Gene from 1975. His hair was the same as it was now, thick and sticking up high on his head, except that in this photograph it was still all brown. He had the same trim physique as he had now and the same smile. If she had met him then, she would have found him sexy. And now that she had seen this picture, she knew that Gene was an attractive man. She hadn't been sure about this before.

A while ago, Muriel had promised Irving, that courtly, neat, little Chinese man, that she would go to the next dance with him. But now she told Gene that he could come along to the dance, too. She would dance some dances with Irving, because she had already promised him that she'd go with him, but she would also dance some of the dances with Gene. She and Irving had never been a couple. They were just dance partners. He had been very patient with her considering that she had not danced in years. Irving had no romantic designs on her, she was sure.

For the occasion, Gene bought a new pair of shoes, shoes with leather soles, which could slide over the wooden dance floor. He looked very cute to Muriel, dressed up in nice slacks and a sweater. Once Flora had pointed out to her that short men could be every bit as attractive as tall men, she had seen that it was true.

Before they left for the dance, Gene presented her with a gift. It was a silver and turquoise pendant in the shape of a butterfly, and it went perfectly with what she was wearing—a white sweater and a flowered skirt which would swirl around her knees when she danced, as she was passed back and forth between Irving and Gene.

When Muriel was dancing with Irving, Gene danced with another woman who was sitting at their table. Everyone seemed young and attractive. The band was playing all the old standards— "Begin the Beguine," "Ojos Verdes," "Hernando's Hideaway." Then she was dancing with Gene, and she saw the person he had been in 1975. He was smiling so happily and holding her so close, she said, "Don't hold me this close. What will people think?" He answered, "Look around. Everyone's dancing close." And she saw everyone on the dance floor was dancing cheek to cheek.

When the evening was over, the woman Gene had danced with when Muriel was dancing with Irving came over to him and asked, "Do you have your car here?" He said no, and she said, "Come on, then, I'll give you a ride home," but he answered, "No thanks, I'm going home with her, tonight." *Her* was Muriel. Gene seemed to want everyone to know that they were now a couple.

The next day, they packed up her car with overnight bags, and drove to the Gold Country. They took her car because all he had was an old truck. She would drive on the first leg, over the freeways and highways, and he would take over once they got into the mountains, the last thirty miles when the way was narrow and winding. They had been invited to stay for two nights at the home of his old neighbors, and they would also visit his sister while they were there.

Muriel was just happy to be in the car driving, heading out to an unknown destination, asking herself as they passed little villages and country towns, "What if I lived there? What would it be like if I lived here?" She liked looking at farms and fields as the road led deeper into the interior of the mountain, to the roof of the world.

Gene told her that he had met his wife when he was in high school, when he was a senior and she was a freshman. She had been just a kid to him then. After high school, when he was just eighteen, he had enlisted in the Navy, and he had been shipped off to Hawaii where he learned to work with sheet metal on ships. It was before Hawaii was a state, and everyone living there was Asian and Polynesian. While he was in Hawaii he never went on a single date. Then the Japanese attacked Pearl Harbor, and he was pulling bodies out of bombed-out ships. After that, he was shipped back to Alameda, the shipyard across the bay from San Francisco, and soon he got a furlough to go home. While he was there, he ran into the woman who would become his wife, who had been just a kid in high school when he left. She was a woman now, and very pretty. He asked her if she'd come back with him to Alameda, and she said she wouldn't do that unless they were married, so he married her. They had never even been out on a date.

They had four children together, and one of them died. You never get over losing a child, Gene said. Gene and his wife were never totally compatible, he told Muriel. They were not nearly as compatible as Muriel and he were. It was so wonderful, he said, that Muriel and he liked to do all the same things. He had been married to his wife for over sixty years, and he had been faithful to her, but that was then and this was now.

Now Gene was behind the wheel, and suddenly they were enclosed by the pine forest on each side of the road, and the road was a ribbon unwinding before them. All the other cars disappeared, and it seemed like they were the only two people left in the world. Great banks of clouds were climbing into mountains of their own, heavenly, snowy white mountains, outlined in gleaming silver.

At last they came to Gene's friends' place, where they were expected. It was a beautiful wood and glass house in the midst of the forest. Muriel stepped out of the car. The pine needles released their scent, there were jays hopping in the trees, and a hale man with a trim white beard was coming out of the front door smiling. Behind him, a woman wearing a gray jogging suit followed, her white hair in a low ponytail. The man, it turned out, was an executive at GM. This was their vacation home. They had been neighbors of Gene and his wife for many years. They clearly thought very highly of him.

Muriel knew what this was. It wasn't just that Gene wanted her to know him, to be able to imagine his past life. It wasn't simply that he wanted her to see the place where he had lived, although that was also true. He was also proving to her that he was classy enough for her, that he was respected by classy people. These were his character references. He was making his case, and he was covering all the bases.

Then Muriel thought how it might be her Gene was showing to his old neighbors, rather than the other way around. Perhaps he had brought her to see if they would approve of her. After all, these people must have been friends with Gene's wife. Perhaps this woman and Gene's dead wife had been close friends, canning berries together in the summers and drinking tea by each other's fireside in the winters while quilting.

Gene had done all the cooking when his wife was sick. Now he had been cooking for Muriel ever since their first night together. She loved that he did this. She had cooked meals for Jack almost every night for sixty-four years. That was approximately 23,360 meals. This was the first time in her life since she had left her mother's house that anyone had ever cooked meals for her. It was completely wonderful. He made the bed first thing in the morning and kept everything shipshape. Muriel wondered if these old neighbors, these old friends of Gene and his wife, were glad for him now that his long years of caretaking labors were over, that he had been vouchsafed a bit of happiness. Truly, they did seem happy for him and welcoming to Muriel.

Soon, they would have to go to sleep, but where? Were their hosts going to give them two different rooms out of propriety, or were they going to be given a room of their own? If they were given a room of their own, would there be one bed or two?

"I'll show you where you'll be sleeping," the woman said, and led them down the hall. She opened the door. There was an old fashioned four-poster bed inside covered with a handmade patchwork quilt. There were flowers in a jar on top of a rustic table. A Swedish pellet stove sat in one corner. A door led through the wall opposite to a bathroom. Muriel caught just a glimpse of the claw foot of a bathtub. A window with a gingham curtain tied back on each side overlooked the forest.

One room had been provided. These decent people had assumed they would be sharing a bed. They accepted the idea completely. Then so did Muriel.

Chapter Thirty-one

Flora and Jonah were invited to a sixtieth wedding anniversary party for their friend Molly's parents. Molly and her husband Andrew were old friends. They had met Molly's parents many times over the years, but they were not more than acquaintances. So they were a little surprised they had been invited, although they were glad to come. Flora had heard that Molly's father had developed Alzheimer's, and that his progress downward had been steady, but slow. So this event would be poignant.

When Andrew called to invite them, he explained that they had wanted to make a celebration for Molly's parents' anniversary, and at first they had thought they could just invite Molly's parents' friends. But then they realized they didn't have any more friends—they had all died. So Andrew and Molly decided to expand the scope of the event—now it was a celebration of love over time. It was for Molly's parents, but also for all their friends who were in long-term relationships, and Jonah and Flora were certainly in that category.

"Don't dress up," Jonah said, when they were getting ready to go. "These are Zen Center people."

Molly and Andrew were Buddhists, and most of their other friends were from the Zen Center. Zen Center people always dressed in tasteful garments made of natural fibers. They wore sensible shoes, the women didn't wear makeup, and they let their hair go gray. Flora would wear black linen pants with pockets and a drawstring waist, and a black linen shirt-jacket with three large buttons down the front. Her hair wasn't gray, and it wasn't natural, either. It was streaked with blond.

Flora and Jonah were not Buddhists, of course—even though some of their best friends were—but they enjoyed being in a

Buddhist atmosphere once a year for a few days. So every August they went to Tassajara, Zen Center's monastery in the mountains which operated as a resort in the summer. Tassajara began as a hot springs resort popular in the 1890s. Zen Center acquired the property in the 1960s, and they built a stunning meditation hall, and an elegant dining room overlooking the creek. They had a lovely flower and vegetable garden, and the vegetarian cuisine was renowned. Everything was tasteful, and it was peaceful—except for the gong summoning people to the Zendo, the chanting, the bells punctuating the service, and the clapper waking everyone up at five in the morning to go to the Zendo. Most of the cabins were without electricity and were equipped with kerosene lanterns. Tassajara was located in the mountains behind Carmel Valley. People usually parked in Jamesburg and took a shuttle over the precipitous one-lane mountain road to the monastery. But Jonah always drove them there himself, even though over the years many people had gone over the side of the road and been killed.

It was there, in Tassajara this August, that Flora would turn sixty—that is, if Jonah didn't drive them to their deaths over the road on their way in, and if she didn't die of something unexpected or something as mundane as a stroke before 12:01 AM on the morning of her birthday. It was there that she would find out if her expiration date was going to come true. It was there that, if she wasn't already dead, she would get into bed next to Jonah on the night before her sixtieth birthday. He would fall right to sleep, and she would stay up reading by the light of the kerosene lantern until she heard the *pok pok* sound made by one of the Zen students who worked on the staff during the guest season hitting one stick against another stick as he hurried past all the cabins. This was the reminder to blow out your lantern, not to fall asleep with it burning. There had been a terrible fire at Tassajara once. The old Zendo that had straddled the creek had burned down. Flora would blow out her lamp, not wishing to die by fire—if she was to die.

And then sometime in the hour or two left before midnight, she would fall asleep. People frequently died in their sleep. That was generally accounted a good way to go. If Flora was to go, that might be the best way.

And what would happen to her mother? Ironically, Muriel was to receive the results of her biopsy on Flora's birthday. The first results they had gotten back were inconclusive, and they had sent the sample down to Stanford. It was the policy of the doctor's office not to tell a patient the result of a biopsy, either positive or negative, over the phone. Muriel would have to go to find out the news without Flora. But probably Gene would go with her. Muriel and he had told each other that if one of them got to the point where he or she needed nursing, neither of them would be a nurse to the other. But surely he would go with her to learn the results of her biopsy. Unfortunately, if Flora woke up alive on her sixtieth birthday, she wouldn't even be able to call her mother to hear the results. There was no cell phone service. There was one public phone, but it was always in use or else broken. And, of course, there was no Internet access. Flora would not be able to speak with her mother until they were on the road home—if she was still alive.

Flora was dying to see what was going to happen, to discover if her expiration date was real. Unfortunately, if it was, she might not get to find out, as there was no guarantee that one could know anything once one was dead. Flora thought about how she would feel if she woke up alive on the morning of her sixtieth birthday. She would be happy, of course. But then what would she feel? She would have to feel what it felt like to be sixty.

She suddenly wondered if this whole belief which she had held for the last twenty-five years, this belief that she would die by her sixtieth birthday, wasn't somehow a wish. Freud had said, after all, that all dreams were wishes. But why would she rather die than turn sixty?

Because turning sixty, passing over the threshold to old age, was more frightening than death. There was no more pretending that one was merely middle-aged once one turned sixty. Sixty was the beginning of the end.

And yet, the end might be far off in the future. One might be old a very long time. Muriel had been old for twenty-seven years so far, and she might very well be old for a lot longer than that. Why was Flora so terrified of becoming old?

She did not want to suffer the disrespect the elderly were generally afforded, of course. She didn't want to be relegated to the sidelines. She didn't want to be discounted and overlooked. She didn't want to be forgotten or marginalized.

She didn't want to be riding in the last car of the train.

She had been talking to a friend recently whose mother had just died. They had flown her back to New York to be buried. On the plane, Flora's friend looked out the window and saw the horizon—the edge of the earth, where it dropped off into nothingness. Then she realized that her mother had been blocking this view.

Wasn't almost every piece of literature, at bottom, about realizing that death was real? Didn't nearly every poem she knew remind us to live fully in response to this reality, to seize the day, to gather our rosebuds while we may? If being flush with the reality of death goaded us to live fully, then old age, when death loomed largest, might be the most profound and fully lived time of one's life.

THEY HAD to cross the Golden Gate Bridge to get to Molly and Andrew's house in Muir Beach. Flora crossed the bridge frequently, and it was always new, always spectacular—the view when she looked east into the bay of Alcatraz and Angel islands, of the stony white city skyline. The skyline of the city when she approached it from the north always made her think of Conrad's description of Brussels in *Heart of Darkness*. He had called it a "whited sepulcher." From the bridge, turning her head to the west, she could see the vast sea expanding to the horizon.

Sometimes fog was flowing through the girders looming in front of her as she drove under them; sometimes the sky was a bright blue. When the light was just right, Flora could see the wild Farallon Islands sticking up on the edge of the sea. Seeing them always made her heart leap. She knew some people had a phobia about crossing bridges, and she thought that was a pity, because crossing a bridge could be such a deep pleasure.

Today the fog was hovering three-quarters of the way up the towers, the huge red Art Deco forms which looked, to Flora, like monumental yet dynamic Chinese gates, one on top of the other. These gates seemed like the gates of a mammoth cathedral, their tops disappearing into the mists of heaven. Flora felt like she was on a spiritual journey.

When they got to Muir Beach they took a road up the cliff, and then followed a fork and parked at the bottom of Andrew and Molly's private road. It was a narrow dirt lane, and it wound around the hill, which beetled over the shore. When they got to the house they went inside to the party, and Flora looked around at all the familiar white heads. It had been several years since she had seen many of these people, and they had all aged. And yet, they all seemed at home, on intimate terms, with that fact. They were intent on being who they were. As Buddhists, they believed that life was suffering, and that all suffering came from desire, and that desire was always the wish for things to be other than they were.

If Flora lived past her expiration date she would aspire to be more like the Buddhists. She would simply embrace her life, just as it was, because that was the only life, in fact, that there was. She wandered from room to room talking with various people, and finally she made her way outside, to the patio. The sea was grave below the house.

Finally, Andrew and Molly called everyone into the living room, where they made a toast with champagne and had Molly's parents cut the cake, her mom holding her firm hand over her dad's shaky one. Then Molly spoke. "As many of you know," she said, "my father has been having some problems expressing himself in recent years, so he won't be making a speech. But what he's still good at, and what he still loves to do, is sing. So why don't we sing one of his favorite songs, 'Row, row, row your boat' in a round?"

She divided the room into three parts, and the first part began to sing: "Row, row, row your boat, gently down the stream," and then the second section started to sing "Row, row, row your boat, gently down the stream," while the first section sang "Merrily, merrily, merrily, merrily, life is but a dream," while the third section sang, "Row, row, row your boat, gently down the stream."

Finally, the first two sections came to an end and stopped, one after another, until all that was left was the third and last section singing "Merrily, merrily, merrily, merrily, life is but a dream."

Flora heard the words, as if for the first time, and all the words rang true.

Chapter Thirty-two

Muriel was flying to Denver to play in the bridge tournament and stay at her friend Fred's house. Gene gave her a ride to the airport in her car. She knew Gene didn't want her to go, but she had planned it before she met him, and had been looking forward to it. At least she had been looking forward to it before she met Gene. For years, going to bridge tournaments had been the activity she enjoyed most, and she assumed it still was. But perhaps it wasn't anymore. Perhaps what she enjoyed most was being with Gene. But why must she choose one over the other? Gene had decided to learn how to play, so he could accompany her when she went to the Bridge Club or a tournament. He could partner up with another beginner on these occasions. She knew Gene was a little jealous of Fred, but she assured him he needn't be—Fred was twenty years younger than her.

And Fred knew it, she added to herself. He had looked her up on the Internet. They were just friends, just bridge partners. There was absolutely nothing to worry about. She did not say anything to Gene about how she had heard Fred outside her room when she stayed with him before, and how she had smelled rubbing alcohol.

Muriel realized she was missing Gene as soon as she got on the plane.

But she liked flying alone, she always met interesting people. She liked the idea that they wouldn't know who she was, so she could be anyone. She didn't have any limitations. That was how it was going to be after she died, just like this. It was possible.

Fred was there to meet her at the airport in his big Cadillac. After she had freshened up, they drove to the hotel somewhere on the outskirts of Denver and were in time for the afternoon game.

She had not been in her seat opposite Fred for very long when she noticed he seemed to be gasping for breath. His balding head with its well-barbered fringe of salt and pepper hair was bending over in front of her. His elbows were akimbo above his head and a rasping sound was coming from his chest.

"Are you all right, Fred?" she asked.

"I'm fine," he said. "I'm just having a little trouble breathing." He looked up and his pale eyes were dim behind his glasses.

The bidding began. Fred gasped and turned red.

"Do you have an inhaler?" the man on Muriel's left now said to Fred.

Fred wagged his hand back and forth and shook his head.

"I think there's a pharmacy on the other side of the shopping center," the man said. "Maybe you better go and get one."

"I'll go with you," Muriel said. What else could she do? "We can sit this game out and play in the evening."

Fred stood up from the table. He was shaky. Muriel followed him out the door to the parking lot. She was disappointed. This was not her idea of a good time. "I'll drive," she said.

Fred handed her the keys and they got in the car. Muriel brought the seat forward so she could reach the pedals. Fred's breathing was loud in her ear. She took off across the parking lot. There was a Chevys, a Chili's, a Starbucks, and a Ross Dress for Less, but she couldn't see any pharmacy.

"Maybe it's in the other shopping center across the highway," Fred gasped, so she maneuvered the car out of the parking lot and headed to the other side of the highway and the entrance to the shopping center. In this shopping center there was a Petco, a Borders, and then finally, at the far end, next to a nail salon, a pharmacy. Muriel parked and they walked inside. She felt everyone staring at them as they made their way to the pharmacist's counter and got in line. She did not like waiting in line. The people ahead of them should have ceded their place to Fred. He clearly needed to see the pharmacist more than they did. Finally, it was their turn, and Fred asked for an inhaler while gasping away.

"I'm sorry, but I can't give you an inhaler without a doctor's prescription," the pharmacist said.

"He can't breathe!" Muriel pointed out.

"I think he better go to the emergency room, then," the pharmacist said.

"I don't know where the emergency room is, and he can't drive," Muriel said.

"I'll call for an ambulance, then," the pharmacist said.

Muriel saw that this was necessary. Fred looked like he was about to expire. She was sorry she had ever come to Denver.

The ambulance was there shortly, and as they loaded Fred on board, Muriel told Fred she'd meet him at the hospital. She would drive his car there. The ambulance driver explained to her where the hospital was and then sped off, sirens blaring.

SHE FOUND Fred in the waiting room of the hospital, lying on a gurney. He was still waiting to see the doctor. Muriel sat down and glanced at a magazine. It was a sports fishing magazine, but that was all there was. Hours passed. Finally they took Fred away, and he disappeared behind a curtain.

Muriel continued to wait until a nurse came and got her, and told her she could see her husband now.

Her husband?

"We need to keep him overnight for observation," the doctor told her when she stepped through the curtain.

"You don't understand," she said. "I'm not his wife. I'm not from here. And I've decided to go back to California if I can change my plane reservation. But my suitcase is back at his condominium. And I wouldn't know how to drive back to his condominium from here. I drove his car here from the bridge tournament, and I don't know where I am now. But I can't stay here."

The doctor and the nurse looked at her blankly. They think I'm his mistress, Muriel thought. And they think it's peculiar that a man should be with a woman twenty years older than he is. She had driven his car down an endless highway and through a maze of strip malls and housing developments to get here, and now they were saying that he needed to be hospitalized. But she wasn't going to explain to them that this wasn't really her problem, that there wasn't anything personal between them, there was only bridge, only the anticipation of how the next game might unfold, only the magic of the cards.

"It's okay," Fred said, from under an oxygen mask. They had given him a shot, and he was sitting up. "I'll just take this oxygen tank with me. We can leave now. If you wouldn't mind driving, I'll give you the directions."

When they got back to Fred's house he went into his room to lie down. Muriel knew he should have stayed in the hospital, but that wasn't her problem. She called Southwest and got on a flight first thing in the morning.

When the morning came, Fred insisted upon driving her to the airport. He took the oxygen tank with him in the car. Finally, when Muriel was sitting and waiting for her flight, alone again, she called Gene. "Listen," she said, "I want this to be permanent."

What she meant by "this" was their relationship. What she meant by "permanent" was forever.

He was overjoyed.

HE KEPT repeating it over and over, after she got home, relishing it, savoring it. As for Muriel, she didn't know what had led her to say it. There was someone inside of her that knew exactly what she wanted and exactly what to do to get it. That person inside her had always been there, but she hadn't felt in communication with her until lately. Ceding control to her—her interior self, the one who knew best and never doubted—had allowed Muriel to feel open and expansive.

Just in time. She was almost dead.

Chapter Thirty-three

Flora was picking up not only her mother at the BART station by the library today, but also Gene, who went everywhere with Muriel now, and Daphne, down from Portland for a visit. They were coming to the city to attend another presentation by the Roxbury Arms at the Hayes Street Grill, where they would be served tea and invited to choose amongst an assortment of delicious desserts, while meeting some of the other distinguished elders who had shown an interest in investing in a condominium in this yet-to-be-built twenty-first-century urban retirement residence.

For some time, Muriel had been expressing an interest in moving to the Roxbury Arms. Flora couldn't understand why her mother wanted to move to such a place. It seemed to her like giving up, but she had finally gone with Muriel to a sales presentation where she learned that former Secretary of State George Schultz and his wife were going to be living in the penthouse of the building.

If George Schultz was choosing to move there, the salespeople were arguing, moving there must be the right choice to make. He, after all, had been in charge of protecting the whole nation. If anyone knew if signing up to live at the Roxbury Arms was the prudent thing to do, he did. But this argument wasn't convincing to Flora. She was a Democrat.

Flora knew one of the main reasons Muriel had wanted to move to the Roxbury Arms was so she could live in a place with a dining room, because she didn't want to eat alone. But now Gene was cooking complete meals for her every night, including dessert, so why was Muriel still showing interest in a place with a dining room? It seemed to Flora that they had the eating part of life all taken care of.

She watched Muriel, Gene, and Daphne in her rearview mirror walking towards the car. They were all eager to see the presentation. The place wouldn't be built for three years, Muriel was explaining, and by the time it was ready, she would be ninety. Surely by then she would have to give up driving, and if she stayed in Laurel Dell she would be stuck up on the hill waiting for the shuttle. "It will be good for me to be in the city," she said. "I'll be able to see Flora every day and take her walk in Golden Gate Park with her."

Hearing her mother say this frightened Flora a bit. Although she enjoyed walking with her mother once a week, she liked walking alone most of the time. It was like a meditation to Flora. She believed that it kept her productive, and Flora needed to be productive, because she knew that at the end of each day there would be an accounting:

What have I accomplished today?

Was one of the few precious days I have on earth spent wisely?

Did I feel its pleasure?

What can I say for myself?

Each day had a momentary visit to a cosmic courtroom waiting at the end of it, where it was weighed and put on trial. But Flora did not tell her mother she needed to walk alone most days. She was ashamed of having this need. She didn't think her mother had a lot of respect for people who had needs. Best of all was to need nothing.

Daphne had flown down, in part, so she too could attend. She was interested in knowing what the twenty-first-century advance in senior living was all about. She also thought she and Flora should try to look after their mother's affairs, as their mother might not know what she was doing. Was this a good investment? Could Muriel afford it? Was this company trying to rip Muriel off and deprive her children of their inheritance? Daphne thought she and Flora should go along to the meeting to take notes.

Gene was along because he went everywhere with Muriel now. "He's my little puppy dog," she had explained. The monthly dues at the Roxbury Arms were going to be four thousand dollars, but that included many meals in the dining room and drinks in the cocktail lounge. Muriel had called the girl who was her liaison to the company to ask about what her dues would be if Gene were with her. Would they be more?

"Not a bit," the girl said. She'd still get the same number of meals or cocktails in the bar. As long as he never stayed more than four nights of the week, it was her condo and no one's business who stayed with her. The girl seemed to think it delightful that Muriel had a lover, and seemed confident that Muriel wouldn't have any problems or conflicts once she moved to the Roxbury Arms.

Muriel was telling everyone about all these interactions with the girl as Flora parked the car in the Performing Arts Garage. The Roxbury Arms would give them a validation for the parking, so Flora didn't have to worry about Muriel fussing about the high cost of parking in San Francisco. They all got out of the car, and Daphne gave Flora a big hug.

While she was hugging her, Flora thought how this might be the last time she would see her sister. Daphne was flying back to Portland that night, and Flora's expiration date was the next week. Flora wondered if she should do or say anything by way of closure with her sister, if they had any unfinished business she should attend to. She should probably finally forgive her sister for the trick Daphne had played on her when she was four or five and Daphne eight or nine. They were making perfume in the backyard, putting flower petals and leaves into bottles and filling them with water. And little Flora had wanted to put a label on her perfume bottle, just like the labels on her mommy's perfume bottles—the bottle of Arpège and the bottle of White Shoulders. Flora wanted the name of her perfume to sound French, she wanted it to be "Madame Frou Frou," but she didn't know how to spell. So she asked Daphne to spell it for her, and Daphne spelled out the letters, "M-a-d-a-m-e S-k-u-n-k. Flora wrote that on the label of her perfume and everyone laughed at her. And Flora thought that if she were to have complete closure with her sister, she would also have to forgive her for torturing her every night in the room they shared as little children by saying "goodnight," and after Flora replied "goodnight," saying "goodnight" again, so that Flora would feel she, too, would have to say "goodnight" again, and so on, and so forth. Flora thought about having closure with her sister, but she didn't want to tell her about her expiration date. If she told her, Daphne might laugh at her. Or, she might become maudlin. There was no predicting. There was no point in mentioning it to any of them.

Flora noticed that Gene was dressed nicely in a sweater similar to a sweater Flora's father might have worn, a thin silk sweater with a grey pattern over a white dress shirt. He was wearing his dancing shoes, his polished brown boots. Muriel was giggling and laughing as Gene held on to her arm. They were laughing about the fact that when Daphne called Muriel on the phone, she always asked, "Is *he* there?"

"What's that you're wearing on your feet?" Muriel asked Daphne. Daphne was wearing bright white sneakers.

"Those are my sneakers!" she said, stopping on the street and starting to take them off.

"What are you doing?" Muriel said.

"I'm taking off my sneakers. I brought my other shoes. You said we were going to walk!" She pulled a pair of black patent leather heels out of her tote bag.

"I'm not criticizing you!" Muriel said. "My children always think I'm criticizing them," she explained to Gene.

"That's one thing about your mother, she's never critical," Gene said.

"Are you talking about our mother?" Flora asked.

"You don't mean our mother," Daphne said.

"Your mother never utters a critical word," Gene said.

Flora saw that he was gaga, head-over-heels in love with their mother, so much so that he wasn't even aware of when she was criticizing him. He just knew it felt wonderful, whatever she was doing. That's how their father had been about their mother.

Gene rambled on as they made their way toward the restaurant: He just never expected that things were going to go this way, he said. He thought his life was just about over. Now he just enjoyed every day. Their mother had taken him to so many new places. He and she were just living each day, and each day was a new day and was not like the last day. After all, there was no tomorrow. Today was all they had. And it was pretty great. He had never expected this to happen.

There was possibly no tomorrow for Flora, either, but had she been living that way?

Muriel giggled, and reached for Gene's hand. The restaurant was only a block away and they were the first to arrive. Two lovely young women from the Roxbury Arms were there to greet them. They had the whole back room of the restaurant, which was closed to the public between lunch and dinner. Flora wondered if they would be the only people coming, if other people were too smart to come.

They sat down and ordered their desserts. Flora asked for only tea, afraid to eat anything. Muriel ordered the hot fudge sundae, and Daphne ordered the chocolate cake. It was brave of her, Flora thought, to eat cake in front of their mother.

They were just digging into their treats when another old couple came with their middle-aged daughter, and a third couple arrived who announced that they had never had children. They were unencumbered, they explained with self-satisfied smiles. While they were all eating, the young women held up boards showing the plans for the Roxbury Arms and launched into their sales pitch. They showed them on the plans where the dining room and the cocktail lounge were to be, and explained that there would be a lobby with a concierge and an exercise room. They had two other rooms, and they wanted their guests today to make suggestions for what these might be used for. A library? A game room? A lecture hall?

How paltry this all sounded to Flora compared to Laurel Dell, which had several clubhouses with all kinds of rooms for different activities, a dance floor, a library, a theater, and a computer room.

She hoped her mother realized how much less the Roxbury Arms offered than her current place. The other couples around the table were clearly in the exploratory stage, too. She wondered if either of the other couples would be convinced by this presentation.

"Any questions?" the young presenter asked the group, who were busy with their desserts.

"I have one," Flora said. "What is going to be so twenty-first century about the Roxbury Arms?"

"That's an excellent question," the young woman replied. "What will distinguish us is based on the extensive research we have done. We have discovered that people don't like to be moved out of their homes when they need assisted living. So if you should ever need nursing care, you will be able to stay in your own condominium, and home healthcare workers will come to you."

"Is the cost of that included in our monthly fees?" the daughter of the couple sitting next to Daphne asked.

"We will coordinate these services for you, certainly," the young woman said, "but you would have to pay the fees for the care directly to the worker. However, we will be able to find the very best people."

"THEN WHY not just have Emilio come to your own home in Laurel Dell, and get care there without moving, if you need it?" Flora asked as they were walking back to the car.

"For four thousand dollars a month, you and Gene could come to the city and stay at a nice hotel here whenever you wanted," Daphne said.

"And you wouldn't have to live in two rooms," Flora said.

"I just thought that in three years I might be ready to move," Muriel said. "I'll be ninety!"

Mom, don't be afraid, Flora wanted to say. I know it's a scary number, like sixty. But you show no sign of slowing down. Your beauty has not dimmed, it has seemed to increase. You're in a relationship with a nice guy, and you're having a lot of fun with him. You should just relax and allow yourself to be happy, Mom.

There's nothing to worry about, only the whole world to enjoy every day.

But what about me? Have you even given a thought to the fact that next week I will turn sixty, if I don't die first? Mom, I'm scared to death of turning sixty. And I'm scared to death that I won't.

But Flora didn't say any of this out loud to her mother. What was the point? Her mother would think that she was insane.

One thing she was thankful for was that she didn't feel she needed to have closure with her mother. Ever since her parents had moved to Walnut Creek, Flora had been growing closer and closer to her mother. Whereas before she had been wary of spending time with Muriel, because she somehow always came away from these encounters feeling bad about herself, that had changed in the years Muriel had been in the Bay Area. Now Flora looked forward to her visits with her mother and thoroughly enjoyed them. She had begun to see her mother as a phenomenon. She was very proud of her. Her mother was driving, she was independent, she had all of her marbles. Flora couldn't bear the idea of her mother living in what amounted in the end to a "home." A "home" was for people who were on their way out, and Flora couldn't bear to think that her mother might be in this category.

That thing growing in her arm might be about to do her in, Flora knew, but somehow she didn't really believe that it would. That's why she wasn't overly worried about being down in Tassajara when Muriel went to the doctor to get the news. Flora knew it was irrational, but she believed her mother to be immortal. If she allowed her mother to move to a place like the Roxbury Arms, a last resort, a senior residence of which there was none more senior, it would be tantamount to accepting that Muriel inevitably would die, and to accept that was to allow it to happen.

Chapter Thirty-four

Muriel had a long list of things she wanted to do while she still could, like visit Coit Tower and ride the ferry to Angel Island. Visiting Alcatraz had been on the list, but then she finally went there one day when Daphne was down for a visit. The ferry ride to the penal island was glorious, and the prison quite horrifying. She had enjoyed it.

Today when Flora picked up her and Gene at the BART station, they drove to the Sutter-Stockton Street garage, parked the car and walked up Grant Avenue to Washington. Today they were all going on the Chinatown walk, something she had wanted to do for quite a while. She had first seen brochures for the city walks in the library, which sponsored them. They were free and led by knowledgeable guides. She and Flora had been on one in the Mission District where they had seen and learned about all the murals; and she had been on another walk with Daphne that explained about the history of the buildings on Market Street. After each one, she had sent the library a check for a generous, tax-deductible donation.

Muriel was fascinated to learn the arcane details of the history of the city. The personable guides on these walks always explained what was not obvious to the naked eye. Most people walked the streets of the city without seeing half of what was there. Muriel wanted to know about it all, so she could experience everything as fully as possible.

The walk began in a square in the heart of Chinatown. Most people didn't know that this was the original site of city hall, their guide explained. Nor were they aware that if they dug under the streets of the city, they would find bedsteads and couches and tables and the hulls of ships.

During the gold rush, ships had poured into San Francisco Bay. Their hulls were used as landfill so the city could expand. In fact, everything was thrown into the bay for this purpose, including furniture and even pianos which had been pushed from the windows of the whorehouses and lavish mansions overlooking the wooden ship-hull ground rising beneath them.

Their guide told them this, and then he led them away from the tourist Chinatown, to the real Chinatown, and they saw a fortune cookie factory. Muriel gave her sample cookie to Gene. Then they saw a Taoist shrine and an herb shop, and Flora said to Muriel, "Mom, remember when that Russian man gave you those Chinese herbs to boil for Dad?"

She didn't remember.

"They tasted bitter, but Emilio boiled them and served them to Dad. They were like pieces of bark and roots," Flora said, but that didn't jog her mother's memory. "And that Russian man used to give Dad special massages," Flora said.

Muriel didn't remember that either.

"He said he might be able to get Dad to walk again, because there was nothing wrong with his legs. But the switch in his brain which set everything into motion was broken. And that switch might be fixable. And it might not."

It hadn't been. Muriel didn't remember any of this. It was so long ago, in another lifetime. Who knew she was going to have another lifetime?

After the Chinatown walk they went to Greens for lunch.

"I lived in the mountains twenty years," Gene said to Flora as they waited for their food. "I built that house up there myself. The air was so pure and the night sky so filled with stars and the water from our well so sparkling that we could have gone on that way forever, square-dancing with the neighbors once a week. But the wife got sick, and we came down here, and I never would have guessed I'd be here, looking out at the Golden Gate Bridge."

"Isn't the view amazing?" Muriel said. Sharing the view with Gene made it twice as wonderful.

"Did you ever hear your mother snore?" Gene asked Flora.

Muriel would get him for this.

"I sure have," Flora said.

"It's a distinctive sound," Gene said.

They were ganging up against her. But Gene was also letting Flora know that he and she were sleeping together. It made her laugh. Gene was always announcing to people in one way or another that they were sharing a bed. Just the other day he had come with her to play at the bridge club with another beginner, and she had overheard someone ask him if he also lived in Laurel Dell, and he had turned and pointed at Muriel and said, "I live with *her*."

In the Greens dining room the light was blond beneath the high rafters, among the huge lacquered-wood tree-stump and sea-wrack Noguchi sculptures. On the walls there were huge tempera paintings of vegetables that were somehow very, very sexy.

"What do you hear from Daphne?" Flora said.

"If it weren't for your sister, we'd never know when to get up in the morning," Gene said. "We were lying there this morning wondering when to get up when the phone rings, and it's her."

Muriel laughed. Daphne called her every day. Gene was telling Flora again that he and she woke up together every morning. He was bragging! Strutting like a little rooster.

After they had finished their lunch, Flora drove them back to the BART station. "So, shall we make a date for next week?" Muriel asked, before getting out of the car.

"I'll be in Tassajara next week," Flora said.

"Right, I forgot," Muriel said. Then she thanked Flora for a wonderful day, and she and Gene started to get out of the car.

"Give me a kiss goodbye," Flora said.

That was odd—Flora had never asked Muriel to kiss her goodbye before. She already had the car door half-open, but she leaned back and kissed her daughter on the mouth. Then she

189

got out and crossed the street holding Gene's arm, and they went down the escalator into the BART station.

It was while she was going down the escalator that Muriel remembered that Flora's birthday was next week, and she hadn't wished her a happy birthday. What a terrible mother she was, forgetting her daughter's birthday. But Flora hadn't mentioned it. She would have to send her a card. She would do it tomorrow.

"I think I'm getting Alzheimer's," she said to Gene. "I completely forgot my own daughter's birthday." But this was a dissimulation. She didn't really believe she was getting Alzheimer's. She knew there was another reason why she hadn't remembered it.

It was because that day had another, new significance, one that had obscured her daughter's birthday. It was the day Muriel would get the results of her biopsy, the day she would find out if she was going to live or she was going to die. She should be forgiven if she temporarily forgot her daughter's birthday. She had forgotten because Flora's birthday was falling on a day Muriel had been trying to forget, a day she was afraid to think about.

Chapter Thirty-five

It was morning. The day stretched ahead of Flora to where it ended at midnight, when she would be no more, when she would be struck down. When the clock struck twelve and the calendar page flipped up it would reveal Flora's sixtieth birthday, the first day of her death.

Or so she thought. Flora and Jonah were on the Tassajara Road. It was terrifying—a narrow, rutted, one-lane dirt road balanced on the side of a mountain. Flora was trying not to look at the way the road was dropping away in front of them. These mountains, with their nearly vertical sides, reminded her of a Chinese painting.

To keep herself from looking at the frighteningly precipitous way the mountain fell away from the edge of the road, she concentrated on looking down at the road, and focused on looking for giant pinecones. She had a collection of them she had helped herself to over the years. The pinecones were so large and so beautifully made she couldn't get enough of them. And they were free. She called them "doozers," and "lalapaloozers."

Was this really her last day on earth, or was that an illusion? This mountain they were driving over seemed real, but it also was only an idea of a mountain, a Chinese painting she was inside of. Perhaps she was only a brush stroke on an ancient Chinese painting hanging in the hall of an emperor.

They were on this road for an hour, and the adrenalin left over from the hair-raising ride was still coursing though Flora's veins when they arrived. Every detail of the landscape was clear to her—the rocky mountain rising and falling on all sides, the trees growing straight up into the stratosphere, the yuccas with their deadly sting balancing their yellow blossoms on the tops of their sudden stalks.

Jonah parked and they unloaded their luggage into a cart, and Jonah pushed the cart over the half-moon bridge and into Tassajara. Maybe on this visit Flora would go to the morning meditation. She had always wanted to see what it was like. Tomorrow morning would be her birthday, and if she woke up alive at five when the monk in his black robes passed by their cabin knocking his stick against another hollow stick, she would go to the meditation hall, remove her shoes, and enter the hall smoky with incense where kerosene lanterns lit the alters from which the Buddhas smiled down, amused.

Their cabin was the second one over the bridge, the simple cabin they always stayed in. But it had been modernized since they were here last. There were new windows with screens and there was electricity in the bedroom now—although there was still a kerosene lantern in the bathroom. Flora didn't like these changes. They made the simple and primitive and Zen-perfect effect seem like a sham.

Just when they had finished unpacking, they heard the bell sound for lunch, so they made their way to the courtyard and retrieved the napkin rings labeled with their names. Other guests milled around the courtyard, chatting. Everything was as it always was when they came here, but something was missing. The same jays swooped down and up to the roof of the kitchen and into the trees in the courtyard. Squirrels darted here and there, but something was off.

It was the sound of the creek rushing beneath the dining hall. Flora walked to the edge of the courtyard and looked down. The creek was almost completely dry. Here, as all over the earth, the weather had been getting steadily warmer and drier each year.

It was one thing to accept that her own life might be ending, but the whole world? The whole world was coming to an end. The raging creeks with their endlessly full rushing sounds were being silenced. Silence was invading the earth, and in that silence her last heartbeats would be echoing. It was very hot, and the heat caused Flora to move slowly. After lunch, they would take a nap and then go to the baths.

Zen Center had replaced the old mineral baths with a beautiful new Japanese-style bathhouse with a men's side and a women's side, each with a plunge full of healing mineral water, a large deck, and an outside pool to soak in, with a path down to the creek where, after soaking, one could refresh oneself in the cold water. But this year there was almost no water in the creek to refresh oneself in. Moreover, all the water in Tassajara was being rationed, a monk told them, coming to their table while they ate their lunch.

It was odd being here without the creek sound, Flora thought. The sound of the creek had held everything together, it had been the glue that made everything everything. Now there were only disparate parts.

On the way back over the bridge to the cabin, something stung Flora on the arm behind her armpit. It was either a hornet or a bee—she saw it and heard it buzzing as it attacked her, but she couldn't tell what it was. It looked ragged to her, an insect which had become scruffy in its battle for survival. The sting was enormously painful, and she cried out so that Jonah, who had gone ahead of her into the cabin, would come to her aid.

The pain was terrible, but it was bearable because it was not pervasive. It was localized in one spot. She wondered if it was a wasp or a bee. The difference was that the bee left its stinger in you, sacrificing itself for the greater good—or was it the wasp that did that? Could a bee live without a stinger? Lately, all the honeybees had been disappearing. Why were they disappearing? Were they going crazy, and just stinging people randomly until they were all stinger-less and so soon dead and gone—as Flora would be, within a matter of hours?

Maybe this was how it was happening—her day cut short at two in the afternoon, deprived of her last ten hours. Death from a bee sting. Soon she would be going into anaphylactic shock.

But was she really allergic to bee stings? She did not believe that she was. Yet when was the last time she'd had one? She couldn't remember. Had she ever had one? Perhaps not. This one hurt like hell. Finally, Jonah arrived.

"What is it? What is it?"

"A bee stung me."

"Let me look. Yes, the stinger's still in."

"Get it out!"

"Hold still. There—got it. It's a big one!"

"It still hurts!"

"I got it all out. Come on inside. Maybe you should lie down. Should you put something on it?"

"What?" she asked. She hadn't brought any medicines with her. There were remedies she had heard of—meat tenderizer or mud—but where would she get meat tenderizer? And she wasn't sure she wanted to smear herself with mud. She slipped out of her shoes and lay down on the bed. She wondered if there might be a box from a jeweler under her pillow. Jonah always surprised her with presents under her pillow on her birthday, their anniversary, and Valentine's Day.

"What about calamine lotion?" he said.

"I don't have any calamine lotion, and I don't think it does any good, anyway," she said.

"Isn't there anything we can do about it?" he asked, standing over her solicitously.

"I don't think so. On the other hand, I don't seem to be going into anaphylactic shock."

So, this wasn't it. This was a false alarm, a little joke of God's. She still had ten hours left. "I guess I'll go to the baths," she said.

"I'll go, too," Jonah said.

THEY WALKED hand in hand down the path bordering the creek to the bathhouse. Jonah went left to the men's side, and Flora to the right for the women. She removed her shoes, stepped onto the deck, and turned right at the little shrine with the Buddha and fresh flowers.

Inside, she went to one of the hooks on the wall and undressed. A few other women were dressing and undressing, and she snuck glances at them. It was so strange that each person was encased in a body, in a particular bag of skin. She avoided looking at her own naked body in the mirror in case the sight would distress her. But why not look, why not see what had contained her all these years? She stood at the vanity mirror and looked at her breasts. Those breasts had been the location of a great deal of delight to her, and unlike the bee sting whose effect had stayed local, the sensations her breasts had experienced over the years had begun in their nipples and had radiated out into her entire body and then into the entire world. She was grateful to her body, flawed as it was, for all the pleasure it had afforded her. She was going to miss it desperately.

She was grateful to it also for all the pleasure it had given her walking. Walking, simple as it was, had turned out to be something she wanted to do almost every day of her life.

Flora walked outside to the outdoor pool, which was just large enough for four people. There were already two naked women in it, one older than her and one younger. Flora climbed into the rock-walled pool—slowly and carefully, because the water was very hot. It felt very good, so soothing and comforting that she soon lost all self-consciousness about her naked body, except for the consciousness that she had lost her self-consciousness.

The woman who was younger than Flora was somewhere between thirty-five and fifty. Her body looked untouched, as if no man had ever caressed it. It was white and slight, and she had small incidental breasts. The other woman was somewhere between sixty and seventy-five, her white hair upswept in the back in an old-fashioned way. She had comfortable breasts, but a stomach that was large and slack and round like a sagging balloon, as if she had been married long and happily and had had many children.

The women were talking about the meteor shower which was to take place that night—shooting stars rushing through the atmosphere and then extinguishing, flaming and burning out, as she would. Flora leaned back against the side of the pool, listening to the women talk and looking up at the tree overhead, its broad leaves quivering in the slight breeze, and the bright blue sky above the tree, the floor of heaven. She didn't want this moment ever to end.

Afterwards, scrubbed fresh, her skin rosy from the heat of the water, she walked down the path a little ways and looked over at the creek. The creek was green, emerald green in some shallow pools caught in the rocks. Across a bridge that had been chained off was the crumbling cement of the old bathhouse. It was a rotting carcass.

Her own carcass would begin to smell quickly in this heat. Was this the end, now? What about her children? Yes, they were twenty-two and twenty-four—almost twenty-five—old enough to take care of themselves, as Flora had been told they would be when she had stood before the cosmic court. But Flora so much wanted to see their lives as they unfolded. She wanted to be there when they needed someone to be there for them. Flora turned and walked back to the cabin, where she found Jonah asleep on the bed.

She decided not to take a nap herself because she didn't want to miss one moment of this day. She hung her towel on a peg and waited for Jonah to wake up.

Outside the dining room in the plaza before dinner, Flora saw the two women she had seen in the bathhouse. They were walking around as if they didn't have this secret under their clothes, their naked bodies. She thought about the custom of washing bodies before burial, the tenderness with which it was done. She looked around at the table where the napkin rings were laid out. Hers wasn't there. Was she already a non-person?

They lingered over tea after the meal was over. Was there anything she needed to tell Jonah? No, nothing. He knew everything. He was in her head and she was in his head. She would live on in him after she was gone.

They went back to the cabin. Flora thought she could hear the creek, faintly, beneath their window, struggling to rush forward. She turned out the electric light. Jonah took her in his arms and she melted into him, holding back her cries because the walls were thin, and other cabins were all around. If this was the last time she was ever to make love she would have preferred to be allowed to scream, but it wasn't really a significant constraint. Ecstasy was ecstasy, with or without screaming.

It amused Flora that her last act was turning out to be an act of politeness, this refraining from screaming in deference to other people who might not wish to hear it.

No, that wasn't true. What was she thinking? Her last act was the act of love.

Jonah was already asleep.

Flora did not want to fall asleep. She did not want to miss anything. She wanted to see it coming when it came. It was already eleven. It would have to be a stroke—the stroke of midnight—unless it wasn't coming.

IT WAS completely black. Flora could see nothing. There was no moon, no light reflecting into the heavens.

She thought about the cosmic courtroom, her trial before the heavenly court. She remembered the wainscoting and the calendar pages. She remembered the word "docket." She remembered how her dead relatives had failed to come to her defense. What was there to defend? Everyone was scheduled to die.

FLORA AWOKE with a start. She had let herself fall asleep for a split second. She must make a better effort to stay awake.

Out of the blue she remembered something she hadn't remembered since the night of the dream—if it was a dream—when she was pregnant with Lulu, twenty-five years ago. She remembered that immediately after she had visited the heavenly court, the dream cut to a new location, high in the Himalayas where the air was very pure and thin, and the mountains rising all around were blue-tinged chalk, and it was here that Flora found herself.

She was sitting in a monastery quite comfortably in a cross-legged posture on the dry stone floor. She was wearing the red velour bathrobe she wore when she was pregnant with Lulu because it tied with a belt and was large enough to contain her belly. She had continued to wear that robe for several years after Lulu was born, until it was so threadbare she had to replace it. She had been sorry to let it go; it was so soft and warm, and its deep red color had always pleased her. It was nice to think that she would have it again to wear through all of eternity. It covered her knees and spread out behind her on the monastery floor.

She was sifting dust.

Sifting dust was the exact right thing to do, the most satisfying and basic action in the universe.

She was both inside and outside this scene.

Outside the scene she was saying to herself, I will be content if this is how I end up spending all of eternity.

Inside this scene, here in the monastery, she sits effortlessly in a half-lotus position she has never before mastered. She is focused neither on the visual field nor on the darkness behind it.

The sheer gravitas of the mountains is holy.

Her eyes are half-closed, yet the universe is so vast that it is there even in the corner of her eyes—the bleached white mountains towering all around, above and below her. Out of the bones of one of the mountains, the monastery in which she sits has been carved. All is clear, all the tiny crevices of the mountains made of bones.

She sees every hairline fracture of the stones beneath her legs and upturned bare feet. The room she is sitting inside has no roof. Her hands rest lightly in her lap, one inside the other; their open palms face upwards. They are as perfectly rendered as the white hands emerging from the elaborate jeweled sleeves of a woman in a Dutch Renaissance painting hanging in a gilded frame in the Uffizi Gallery in Florence.

Flora's visibility is unlimited. Others are meditating around her. She is not alone.

Chapter Thirty-six

Muriel sat in the waiting room of the Laurel Dell clinic with Gene by her side. Her appointment was for 10:00, but it was already 10:15. At the opposite end of the room was an old woman, the same one who had been here last time. She was in her same wheelchair, wearing something that looked like a white bathrobe and that also looked like a shroud to Muriel. Her hair was white also, as was her skin. Muriel's hair, which she never dyed, was only half white, still very brown in the front. And her skin was surely not horrifying like this woman's. She took care of her skin. The old horror was calling "Nurse! Nurse!" at the top of her lungs, just as she had before. Did she live in this waiting room?

"We know you're here, Mrs. Gevurtz. Your appointment's not till 10:30. Your driver dropped you off too early," the nurse said in a syrupy sweet but overly loud tone.

"Nurse! Nurse!" Mrs. Gevurtz called again, annoyingly. No matter how long she lived, Muriel would never allow herself to turn into Mrs. Gevurtz, a repellent old crone. She would kill herself first.

"We know you're here, Mrs. Gevurtz," the nurse said, again, a model of patience, perhaps, or more likely, of restrained disdain.

Muriel would not tolerate such disdain. She was not patient. She did not like to be kept waiting. Gene patted her hand. She didn't have to tell him what she was thinking.

"It is what it is," he said.

Finally, she was called into the examining room. To her relief, Gene was allowed to go in with her—perhaps because she was not required to undress. The doctor was not going to reexamine her—he was going to deliver the news. She'd had to wait an unconscionable long time to get the results of this biopsy, because their first analysis was inconclusive. They didn't know what they were doing.

199

She waited in the room for another fifteen minutes with Gene holding her hand in two of his before the doctor appeared, dark eyes flashing in his plump, rosy face with its somber black beard. She had never trusted this doctor. What was he saying?

"The news is that we really don't know what it is, except that it's not a fatty tumor."

How backward was medicine. How little doctors actually knew. It was all a mystery. "Then what can it be?" Muriel asked.

"I can't say for sure," the doctor said, "but I have a theory. I've been reading over your chart. Some time ago you were dragged by a car and suffered two black eyes and a great deal of bruising, but you broke no bones."

"What does that have to do with my arm?"

"May I ask you in what manner you were dragged by the car?"

"My tote bag got caught in the car door when I closed it. My arm was through the handle. My lower arm."

"Precisely. It was your lower arm. You were pulled along by your lower arm. It sustained all your weight, and it didn't break, but the tissue was traumatized. And this is how it reacted. The cells reorganized themselves and grew this large lump. This is where you were touched by the Angel of Death, if you will allow me the metaphor."

"Should I do anything about it?" Muriel asked. "Is there anything to do?"

"I'm afraid all we can do is keep watching it," the doctor said.

WHAT WAS this? She'd been expecting some kind of definitive answer. But at least she hadn't gotten a death sentence—she laughed aloud at that. No, there was no reason to think she wasn't going to continue to live now.

She was alive now. Gene's warm hand was holding hers, and the sensation was delicious. It was delicious to be alive. Gene was smiling at her with love, flirting with her. Gene would be here with her, keeping her company. She was going to live, and she was not going to be alone.